# West of the Pecos

As Tom Dix and Dan Shaw reach the infamous Pecos River, they wonder if the old West they seek might still exist across the river's rippling water. It was said that the law had not yet reached the Pecos valley and the two riders decide to investigate.

But trouble is brewing in the lawless land. Settlers have been sent to tame yet another vast territory, but the ranchers already there decide to make a stand and destroy the uninvited intruders. Pooling their resources, the ranchers send for legendary Matt Blair, one of a rare breed of hired killers known as shootists.

But there is another legendary figure in the Pecos who hates Blair and his sort. He is known throughout the West as Wild Bill Hickok. When the pair finally collide all hell breaks loose.

# West of the Pecos

## WALT KEENE

**A Black Horse Western**

ROBERT HALE · LONDON

© Walt Keene 2003
First published in Great Britain 2003


ISBN 0 7090 7348 8


Robert Hale Limited
Clerkenwell House
Clerkenwell Green
London EC1R 0HT

Typeset by
Derek Doyle & Associates, Liverpool.
Printed and bound in Great Britain by
Antony Rowe Limited, Wiltshire

*dedicated to the memory of*
*William 'Hopalong Cassidy' Boyd*

# PROLOGUE

They said that there was no law west of the Pecos. It was a truth which had cost many innocent men their lives. Yet on the vast ranges that seemed to stretch off into eternity, it was a place where men could discover themselves and lose the past that had dogged their trails. It was one of the last lawless territories left in a land hell-bent on settling every square foot of ground between the eastern and western seaboards.

This was a land into which God had yet to venture and it showed. The sparse dots of civilization were spread so thin that they had become almost invisible amid the more basic requirements put in place at all new frontiers once men rein in and decide to ride no further.

The first men to arrive in any new land were always the merchants, quickly followed by the makers and sellers of liquor. The barbers and gamblers were never far behind. Females of dubious character willing to satisfy men without ever demanding anything except an agreed fee, would appear as soon as the first tent was erected.

The ingredients were always the same and made up what became an average frontier town. This was how all the towns west of the Pecos were. Civilization had no place here for this was a land designed by and occupied by men.

Yet far away and unknown to those who frequented the Pecos ranges, signatures on papers had already signalled the doom of this place.

The Pecos River was long and wide and marked a border that few had the courage to cross. But men did cross over that never-ceasing flow of water. Men who were trying to find something that would make their existence better or those who simply wished to find a place where they could savour the ever-dwindling taste of a more basic existence.

Cattle rustlers did not take long to discover a place where they could drive their herds of stolen steers without ever being followed or brought to book.

The vast open ranges of the Pecos Valley were perfect for fattening them up and making their fortunes. These were not ranchers in the true sense of the word, but men who wanted to create empires that would make them wealthier and more powerful than any other men on the face of the earth.

A handful of powerful men allowed their herds of stock to graze together on the huge range that filled the infamous Pecos valley. There were no fences on this land because there was no need, for thieves do not steal from thieves.

These so-called ranchers had ruled the Pecos by their ruthless might for decades. They had carved out a paradise for themselves because the only law west of the Pecos was gun law.

Supreme and totally unopposed by anyone or anything, they had reigned by their own rules and killed all who dared get in their way. Everyone who dwelled on the untamed ranges were part of the same soiled whole.

There was indeed no recognized law west of the Pecos. But it was starting to creep slowly over the unmarked border. With the blessings of faceless politicians back East, the settlers began to spread ever westward with their covered wagons and plans to settle the heart of the American interior.

But in the exquisite marble halls of power, the men in their frock-coats knew nothing of what lay beyond the Pecos River except that there was plenty of land. Millions of acres of land ripe for settling.

As farmers began to settle the ranges and erect their fences and sow their crops, the powerful ranchers and the men who lived off their backs knew that their very way of life and existence was under threat.

It was a cancer they had to stop spreading at all costs.

The settlers were bringing civilization to a place

that had rejected it for more than a score of years.

The settlers were people who had faith.

They would require every ounce of it to survive.

# ONE

It was a weathered man who stared out across the wide Pecos River silently trying to see beyond the heat haze and bright dancing light that reflected off the shallow water. Tom Dix was a man of many varied talents. He had been a cowboy and a hired gunfighter during his youth. Two very different professions, yet he had excelled in them both. Tom Dix was a man who could be relied upon always to do the right thing and that honesty had cost him dearly.

This river reminded him of another far to the south. A river which he would have been wise to avoid.

For years Dix had been well paid by those who wanted to hire his gun skills, but that had all come to a premature end when he made the tragic mistake of killing a sheriff whilst chasing a ruthless killer through the dark alleys of a small town on the banks of the Mississippi.

With an honesty rare in most grown men, Dix

had returned to the scene of the crime and admitted killing the lawman. It had been a gamble which he had lost. The price of his error was twelve years of his life.

A dozen years spent shackled in chains. It had been an experience that would have destroyed most men but Dix had survived. Against all the odds, he had somehow survived.

Tom Dix stood on the white sand and stared out across the wide shallow river which he knew to be the unmarked boundary that few had the courage to venture across. The sun was noon-high and blazing down upon his shoulders with a ferocity that he knew well from his days riding herd on the Texas panhandle.

The almost blinding sunlight bounced off the slow-moving waters and made the wrinkled eyes squint. Beads of sweat trickled down from beneath the hatband of the weathered Stetson over the man's tanned features.

It was less than six months since he had staggered out of the prison gates into a world that he no longer understood or felt at ease in. He could still feel the shackles around his ankles even though they were long gone. One man had brought him back from the verge of insanity and given him his faith in himself once again.

That man was Dan Shaw. A retired lawman.

Dix could see a land beyond the river which was infamous and yet it seemed totally at odds with its own reputation. He rested his wrists on the grips of his guns and wondered if he might just find a world there that was like the one he had once led before his imprisonment.

It was two months since he and his friend Dan Shaw had left Abilene, seeking a place that would allow them to live out what remained of their lives in peace.

These were men who both came from an earlier age, when things had been so much simpler, and they had decided to try and see if such a place still existed.

Fleeing the civilization that was sweeping across the country and tying people down in lassoes of red tape, the pair had so far failed to find their own personal Utopia. It seemed as if everywhere was now ruled by faceless people with gigantic rule-books. They had encountered thousands of men who did not deserve the name and allowed themselves to be harnessed like mules to time-clocks. Nothing appeared to be the same any longer and they were looked upon as relics of an age that no longer existed.

Their sort were reminders of darker times. Folks like Dix and Dan were not welcome any more.

Yet across the Pecos River it was said that men were still men and the old ways still prevailed. Dix licked his dry lips and moved back to the seated former lawman and sat down beside him.

No two men could have had pasts that were more different than Tom Dix and Dan Shaw, yet they had found that they shared a kindred spirit.

They wanted to find the old West where men were men and withered old women did not wave Bibles in people's faces and try to banish everything interesting from the boundaries of their sanitized worlds.

Towns where men could wear their guns without being ordered to remove them. Towns where you could still find dance-hall girls who were bold enough to paint their lips and powder their faces.

Towns with some blood still left in their veins.

Yet so far they had not found anything remotely resembling the good old days.

Did it still exist? Or had they simply lived too long and were unable to fit into the new way of life?

Dix and Shaw had more than $4000 between them which they had intended to use to buy themselves a small ranch. They were starting to think that they would never find anywhere worth spending a penny of that small fortune on.

Dan Shaw was of a similar age to his partner and yet looked much younger. Unlike Dix, he had not spent twelve years on a chain gang.

'You reckon we'll be welcome over there, Dixie?' Shaw asked. He shook the sand from his left boot, then hauled it back over his moth-eaten sock.

'They say there ain't no law over there.'

The retired US marshal raised an eyebrow.

'Might be wise if we don't mention my past.'

'Yep. Might be best.' Dix grinned. He lifted his canteen off the sand and unscrewed its stopper.

14

The water was just out of the river before them and was cold and sweet. 'Seems to me that most of our problems have been caused by the law, Dan.'

'How come?'

'Well, in every town that we've ridden into since we left Abilene folk have been up to their necks in rules and regulations. Reckon that's the law, ain't it?' Dix screwed the stopper back on the canteen and rubbed the sweat off his top lip.

Shaw nodded in agreement.

'Yeah, too many damn rules. Maybe it is better over there in the Pecos Valley. Can't be no worse.'

'I heard tell that the government has been sending wagon trains into there for the last year or so,' Dix said, staring at the bright water before them. 'I reckon that ain't gonna go down very well with the folks already there.'

'That ain't none of our concern.' Shaw shrugged. 'All I want to do is find us a little spread with a few head of stock on it and no damn four-feet-high petty official telling me what colours I have to paint the roof shingles.'

'How many towns do you figure are over there?' Dix asked.

'I heard that there are three or four towns dotted around the ranges. And not one of 'em has a church.' Dan Shaw grinned widely at his partner.

'That'll make it a damn sight more peaceable than all them towns behind us. Ain't nothing stirs folks up like Bible punchers.'

'I didn't see no churches in Abilene, Dixie.' Dan sighed.

'They had Wild Bill Hickok,' Dix suggested. 'You don't need no church when you got him preaching with them .45s.'

'True.'

Dix lifted his hat from his head by its brim and rubbed the sweat off his temple with his sleeve. Then he placed the Stetson back over his grey hair.

'I just wanna find a town that ain't full of dried-up old women who are jealous of any female worthy of calling herself a real woman.'

'Yeah, it seems like old women have ruined every damn place we've been to over the last couple of months,' Dan Shaw agreed. His mind drifted back to his own deceased spouse. She had been special. He knew that after losing her, he would never find another who even came close.

Tom Dix stood and hung his canteen on his saddle horn and then picked up the loose reins from the sand. He watched as his friend managed to get to his feet and then patted his knees, as if trying to knock the years from the stiffening joints. It seemed to Dix that it was only when they were in the saddle that they could forget that they were no longer young.

'You figure they got old women over there?' There was concern in Dan's face as he posed the question.

Dix stepped into his stirrup and mounted his tall gelding.

16

'Nope. I reckon they'd hang the old crows over there once they started to get all respectable, Dan.'

Shaw chuckled as he lifted his boot and pushed it into the stirrup. He hauled himself up on to the back of the patient horse.

'Now that ought to be a law, Dixie. Hang all females who start nagging.'

Dix looked long and hard at his friend.

'Did your wife ever nag you, Dan?'

'Nope. Not once in all the years we was hitched.'

Tom Dix liked the way his partner's face always lit up whenever he thought about his wife. It was something he knew gave strength to the man.

'Wish I'd had the pleasure of meeting her.'

'She would have liked you, partner.' Dan leaned across and patted the shoulder of his friend.

'I never envied any man except you, Dan.'

Shaw glanced across at the thoughtful face.

'Why envy me, Dixie?'

'You had something I'll probably never have.'

The two men steered their mounts to the water and spurred them into starting the long walk across the Pecos River. It was hotter than hell and both riders knew that there was probably a real good reason for that.

If the land across the river was anything like its reputation, it was not a place for the innocent. Luckily, each in their own way had long lost their innocence and knew exactly what they were heading towards.

17

# TWO

All eyes within the small Pecos Valley town had turned to study the tall rider who eased his magnificent stallion into the wide main street. It was obvious to everybody that this was no ordinary drifter. This man was very, very different. Either by accident or design, this rider bore no resemblance to any other living man.

He was the only one of his kind.

They noted the fringed buckskin jacket that hung over the saddle cantle and the long brown hair which flowed from beneath the flat-brimmed John B. Stetson hat. The drooping moustache that covered most of his mouth was the final clue as to the identity of the stranger within their midst.

James Butler Hickok was a man who knew that his reputation always arrived long before he did. It had been that way for most of his grown days and still counted for something. Few men could boast the colourful life that the tall elegant figure had led over the past two decades, but for the man who

19

had become known as Wild Bill Hickok there was no reason to boast. His fact outstripped any other man's fiction.

War hero, gunfighter, professional gambler and law officer were just some of the occupations at which he had excelled. He had even tried his hand at being an actor alongside his friend, the famous Buffalo Bill Cody, on the New York stage, attempting to capitalize on the scores of dime novels that were being written about him. Yet this had been a short-lived career due to his hard drinking and habit of shooting live ammunition at stage hands and his fellow thespians.

Frontier humour did not travel.

So Wild Bill had returned to the plains upon which he had become famous and used his natural skills to live his life to the full. Few men could equal his ability with his guns or a deck of cards and even fewer did either with such style.

James Butler Hickok was many things.

But most of all, he was that rarest of creatures. He was a living legend.

Hangman's Corner was a town that echoed of an earlier time. A time when men were slowly venturing out into the unknown of the vast American interior unhindered by the burdens of all things respectable. Hickok himself seemed to belong to a bygone age with his long hair and seemingly out-of-date attire. Yet few had the courage to mention the fact to the tall rider who slowed the pace of his mount and studied the buildings along the wide busy street.

He liked what he saw. Lots of saloons and gambling halls.

Only the ignorant ever went up against the awesome James Butler Hickok. The ignorant and the insane. Even now more than two decades since he had first become famous, there were still men who were foolhardy enough to try their luck. To them, what greater prize could there be than beating the legendary Hickok to the draw?

Wild Bill knew that he would find at least one such gun-toting fool within the Pecos Valley because he drew them like flies to an outhouse. He had long ago acknowledged to himself that one day his luck would probably run out, but in the meantime he intended to lose no sleep over it.

Hickok wondered how many foolish men he had been forced to maim or kill with his lethal cross-draw expertise over the years. So many men with so much ambition and so little skill.

Wild Bill had lost count of the exact number.

Few men cut a more dashing sight than Hickok and he knew it. His hooded eyes gave little of his mood away as the slender fingers teased back on the reins.

His was the original poker face.

Hickok allowed the dust-caked horse to stop and then sat silently staring around him at the hundreds of curious faces that had appeared from every doorway and window. Once again he was the centre of attention and that was a place he knew well.

A strange noise filled the air of the main street. It sounded like a hive of bees as the people began to recite his name, over and over again.

Wild Bill Hickok!

Hangman's Corner had earned its name the hard way. Hickok had spotted the huge tree at the corner of the long street. Its broad branches were scarred with the ropes that had been strung over them. Ropes that had administered range justice. There was indeed no law west of the Pecos that bore any relation to that used across the ever-growing United States, but these people had their own unique brand of justice here. It was a swift justice that usually ended with someone having their neck stretched.

That was the way the tall rider liked it.

This was a place that Wild Bill had long considered travelling into, and now he knew exactly why. This town was just one of the few scattered around the vast Pecos Valley and it suited every sinew of his long lean frame. His eyes had lost count of the number of saloons and gambling halls he had ridden past.

This too suited him.

Yet the rider had not spotted anything remotely resembling a sheriff's office and was neither surprised or concerned. He had had his fill of the law back in Abilene and felt refreshed by leaving yet another tin star behind him.

The townspeople of Hangman's Corner watched as Hickok dismounted. There was a strange elegance in the tall lean figure which was uncommon in these or any other parts. He stood beside the magnificent horse and allowed them to study him. They had never witnessed anything like Wild Bill before.

He gathered up his reins and began to walk across the wide street. Each long stride was in itself a performance that he had honed to perfection over the years. He wanted every one of his audience to see him and remember.

They would never forget.

For he knew that even his image could put the fear of God into most men. It was a ploy that had saved him from having to be constantly ready to fight.

They could see the two pearl-handled gun grips poking out from his slender waist. The lethal Colts sat in their hand-tooled holsters which were like no others. Hickok was the supreme expert of the cross-draw and had designed his gunbelt to give him the precise angles he required to pull his weapons from their holsters faster than the blink of an eye.

He tied his reins to a hitching pole and cast his eyes upward.

The boardwalk was filled with men of all shapes, sizes and colours but they parted like the Red Sea when Hickok stepped up from the street.

His glance dried the words in the mouths of his

onlookers. He pushed the swing doors apart, entered the cool interior of the saloon and headed straight at the bar.

People moved out of his way as his long legs strode across the fresh sawdust. There was a hushed silence in the large room.

Hickok raised his boot, rested it on the brass rail, then leaned on the wet counter and stared hard at the rotund bartender.

'A bottle of whiskey.'

The man turned and lifted a bottle of the best liquor off the shelf in front of the large rectangular mirror. Sweat began to trickle down his face as he turned back and presented it to the expressionless Hickok.

'How much do I owe you?'

'On the house, Wild Bill,' the man stammered.

'Much obliged.' Hickok said, touching the brim of his hat. He raised the bottle-neck to his teeth. He pulled the cork from the black glass bottle and then spat it on the floor.

The patrons of the saloon began to muster their courage and start to filter back towards the tall stranger in the buckskin coat and the knee-high boots. Slowly but surely they surrounded the man who eyed them in the mirror as he poured himself three fingers of the amber liquid.

'So it's the back-shooting lawman from Abilene,' a drunken voice piped up from the other end of the twenty-foot-long bar.

A mere few seconds had elapsed from the time

24

the saloon's customers had made their way back to the bar, and their starting to withdraw again.

Hickok downed the whiskey in one gulp, then started pouring himself another. Yet his eyes were neither on the bottle or the glass. They were fixed on the drunken man propped up at the end of the wet mahogany counter-top.

'I ain't a lawman at the moment, friend,' Hickok said. He threw another glassful of the whiskey into his mouth and slowly swallowed.

The man pointed a finger at Hickok.

'I heard about you. Shooting folks in the back and stealing their money.'

Hickok gritted his teeth and poured a third glass of the fiery liquor into the glass tumbler.

'You heard wrong. I never shot nobody in the back and I ain't never stolen nothing from no one.'

The drunken man pushed himself away from the bar and straightened his gunbelt around his middle until the holster was no longer hanging between his legs but resting correctly on his right hip.

He was probably a pathetic sight when sober, a gutful of whiskey had not improved matters, Hickok thought.

'You killed a friend of mine, Hickok,' the man shouted across the distance between them.

Wild Bill nodded and turned to face the man.

'I killed a lot of men. Who was your friend?'

'Black Pete Jackson.' The man staggered

forward with the fingers of his right hand flexing above the deadly Remington.

'I don't recall the name. But I've killed a lot of men that I never knew socially.' There was a deadly tone in the voice of the taller man that seemed to be warning the drunkard to back off whilst there was still time. 'I don't know who you are but I'm willing to kill you if that'll satisfy you.'

'That's mighty big talk for a long-haired woman with whiskers,' the drunk growled, flicking the safety loop off his gun hammer.

'You must really want to meet up with Black Pete again, friend,' Hickok said quietly.

'I ain't scared of you.'

Hickok's hooded eyes flashed at the man. 'You ought to be.'

The man took another unsteady step towards Hickok and then went for his gun.

Hickok did not move a muscle as he watched the shaking hand pull the weapon free of its holster and aim at him. A gasp seemed to go around the saloon as the drunk fired.

The glass beside Wild Bill shattered into a thousand fragments before Hickok drew one of his guns and returned fire.

The bullet hit the man high in his shoulder and sent him crashing over a card-table and landing in a corner. A cloud of gunsmoke hung on the air between them.

Hickok blew down the barrel of his Colt and

then slipped it back into his holster before turning to the terrified bartender.

'Another glass if you please. My friend seems to have broken my other one.'

'Homer ain't dead.' A voice came from one of the men hovering over the prostrate drunk.

As the new glass tumbler was placed before Hickok, he winked at the nervous bartender.

'Sometimes I'm just a merciful old romantic. I hate killing drunks. It's better sport to wait for the fools to sober up and then kill them.'

The man nodded slowly and watched Hickok filling the new glass to the brim.

# THREE

Of all the men who called themselves ranchers on the vast untamed ranges of the Pecos Valley, only one seemed determined to destroy the newly arrived settlers who were fencing off one section of the open land after another.

Cal Harrigan knew how to get what he wanted. He had sentenced more men to death by a wave of his gun barrel over the years that he had dominated the Pecos, than he could recall. But then, he had been there longer than anyone else. Harrigan had been one of the first men to lead his evil followers into the then untamed land.

Lesser men would not have survived what they found when they reached the Pecos Valley. But nothing upon the massive ranges could frighten Harrigan and his army of ruthless outlaws. The Apache had dwelled there for countless generations, but soon found that the white men who invaded their lands were not simply passing through. They were there to stay and wanted every square inch of it for themselves.

With almost military precision, Cal Harrigan had masterminded his men's venomous attacks on the peaceful Apache encampments. He had driven off the Indians within months of his arrival and used his guns to ensure that no one who entered the lawless Pecos Valley after him, ever forgot who was in control.

He had maintained his position for more than twenty years and had never once been challenged.

Harrigan knew that for the first time the settlers had legal papers which offered them protection in theory. This was a new development that troubled the powerful rancher. He had bided his time when the first of the covered wagons had rolled into what he considered his land. Yet in hindsight this had seemed to be the wrong approach, for the prairie schooners had continued coming over the river.

They had to be stopped.

Drastic action had to be unleashed if Harrigan were to be able to reverse the never-ending line of wagons. With his usual disregard for any one else, he had decided that the only way to ensure that they decided to quit his range of their own free will, was to frighten or starve them off.

The last thing Harrigan and the rest of the people who lived on the Pecos Valley wanted was for the army to be sent in to protect the settlers. That was the only reason he had not allowed his gunmen simply to kill the unwelcome intruders.

Terror had been an effective weapon and had seen half the settlers returning back to less daunting land east of the wide river, but it was not coping with the sheer volume of people pouring into the lawless territory. For every homesteader whom Harrigan managed to intimidate, it seemed that a dozen more would arrive to replace them.

For more than a year Harrigan had been fighting an apparently vain battle and was getting more and more frustrated with every new sunrise.

He knew that even with his score of hired gunfighters, he simply did not have enough men to stop the seemingly ceaseless invasion.

Something drastic had to happen.

The subtle approach had not coped with the ever-increasing numbers of settlers. Harrigan knew that to get what he wanted, he had to become far more bloodthirsty, even if it did bring increased risks of the distant authorities sending the army over the Pecos River.

It was the only way of preventing the entire valley becoming nothing more than a collection of fenced-off farms.

That in itself was already beginning to happen, and to men like Harrigan it was something which spelled disaster to not only his way of life, but that of an entire territory.

His territory.

Decisions had to be made and he was the one who made them. He had already gathered in his fellow cattle-owners for an extraordinary meeting.

31

The first such meeting in the history of the lawless land.

Whatever they decided to do, it had to be unanimous.

Harrigan stood on the porch of his house and stared at the pair of fifteen-foot-high poles with the long whitewashed board stretched between them. This was the only marker that told any strangers to the enormous untamed range who owned the sprawling house and outbuildings. It read simply HARRIGAN in bold red paint.

That was enough to ensure that only invited guests ventured up to the large house with its shaded porch.

He glanced to his side and the faces of his men. The sun was still high and burned down on the tanned faces.

Harrigan pointed at the dust of approaching riders. 'They're comin', boys.'

Joe Conway was his top gun and had been with him since the first time that Harrigan had led him and the score of hired killers across the Pecos River, twenty years earlier.

'When you tell 'em to jump, they jump, boss.' Conway grinned as he rested a boot on the wooden decking of the porch.

'They gotta jump if'n I tells them, Joe. Without me, they'd all have starved long ago.' Harrigan ran the tip of a match down the cool white wall and ignited it. He cupped the flame and brought it to the end of his cigar. He sucked in the smoke and screwed up his eyes, then returned his attention to the horsemen, who were getting closer. 'There ain't a spine amongst the whole bunch of 'em.'

Joe spat at the ground and rubbed his mouth on the back of his weathered sleeve.

'You want me to ride over to Hangman's Corner or one of the other towns later and get us some females?'

Cal Harrigan inhaled deeply, then removed the cigar from his teeth and picked the small pieces of dried leaf from the tip of his tongue.

'Yeah, try Murphy's brothel. I heard tell he's had some new girls brought in to replace the ones he dumped down on the desert.'

'Them new girls ought to taste real sweet, boss.'

The two men smiled knowingly at each other. They both wondered how many females had been abandoned out in the merciless desert once they no longer satisfied the customers, who demanded total obedience and nothing remotely similar to the women they knew dominated all the civilized towns and cities over the unmarked border.

There was a good reason why there was not one female in any of the towns along the valley who were older than thirty. It was the same reason why there were also no children in any of the towns.

'Exactly, Joe. Real sweet.' Cal Harrigan flicked the ash from his cigar and then gritted his teeth. His eyes burned as they studied the horsemen.

'We gonna kill them settlers, boss?' Conway asked. He turned his head and watched the dozen or more riders reining in their mounts near the line of water-troughs.

'One way or another them bastards are gonna die, Joe,' the grim-faced rancher said through a line of smoke that filtered between his teeth. 'But it's a job that's gotten too big for just you boys and me to handle on our own. We have to get the other cattlemen involved and make sure that there is as much blood on their hands as there will be on ours.'

'Will they agree?'

'They ain't got no choice.'

Conway watched the riders dismounting.

'We gonna make them do all the dirty work?'

It was a well-aimed question.

'Damn right, Joe.' Harrigan smiled as he stepped down from the porch and waved the cigar in greeting to the other ranchers and their hired guns. 'These boys are gonna do exactly what I tell 'em to do. They ain't got the brains or the guts to refuse me anything.'

Conway adjusted his gunbelt.

'I'll take a buckboard to Hangman's Corner and pick us up some girls, boss.'

Harrigan's smile broadened.

'Two apiece ought to do just nicely, Joe.'

Conway nodded and walked past the other men towards the barn. He knew that by the time he returned with the bevy of females, Harrigan would have concluded his meeting and the ball would have started rolling.

The settlers were doomed.

# FOUR

Poverty had probably killed more people than all the wars put together. It had a way of keeping its victims in their place and then destroying them. Caleb Watkins was a man who had never had much in his forty-two years of existence. For that was what it had been: a mere existence. He had never been anything except dirt-poor and had resigned himself long ago to his pitiful fate.

Then a year earlier everything had altered when hope suddenly entered his drab life. Or had it been a miracle? To men like Caleb Watkins there was little or no hope from the day that they entered the world to the day that they left it.

When he had found out that there were vast tracts of land being given away to anyone who was willing to undertake the long and treacherous journey across the so-called Wild West, Caleb knew that this would probably be his one and only chance to make something of his life.

At last, Caleb Watkins knew that he had something to offer his wife and small eight-year-old daughter. Something more than a life living in filth until premature death finally claimed them as it always did with those who dwelled in the ranks of the terminally poor.

He could offer them hope.

A future.

No longer would they have to live in the dark narrow streets of the great Eastern city amid the squalor and vermin-infested buildings.

Caleb and Bessie had already lost four of their young children. Little Rosemary had been the first of their children to live beyond the age of five and the two caring parents knew that she too was becoming sickly. There was no colour in the faces of those who lived in the shadows. It seemed that everyone looked like corpses there.

But Caleb had managed to win his ticket to freedom. He was the kind of person whom the authorities wanted to help settle the wilderness. A man with a wife and child who knew how to work with his hands. A man who was so poor that he would appreciate anything he was given, however little.

Caleb had been allocated a hundred acres of fertile land somewhere in a place he had never even heard of before. All any of the successful applicants had been told of their eventual destination was that it lay west of the Pecos River.

He had been given a covered wagon and provisions to settle an untamed land that was being opened up for the good of the ever-expanding country. A small allowance was also to be paid to the settlers when they arrived. They had been told that there was a small trading post where they could get a few luxuries.

What they had not been told was that the trading post lay in the heart of the infamous Hangman's Corner. A town that was filled with people who despised them.

Caleb Watkins had thought that they only had to endure the hardships of the long journey to their new home. A thousand miles meant nothing to a man who had never set foot outside the slums that had spawned him. All he cared about was being free. Being free to breathe fresh air and grow his own food on his own land. Even if he had known that there were men who did not want them on the Pecos Valley, he would still have come.

Seeing his wife and daughter growing healthy and strong in a land filled with others the same as themselves, was more than he could have dreamt possible twelve months earlier. Caleb had been given a precious gift which he would not relinquish.

To simple people like them, this was paradise. There was no other word for it.

Caleb had arrived in the Pecos Valley exactly two months earlier and had hastily built a small house with the aid of his fellow settlers. He in turn helped his neighbours. He had obtained a milk cow and calf and already could see the fruits of his labours growing through the fertile soil.

For a man to see colour filling the cheeks of his small family for the very first time, it was as if he had been blessed by a miracle.

But not he nor any of his many neighbours had known of the dangers which lurked across the huge range that they were slowly and innocently cultivating. They had all thought that apart from the small trading post the entire valley was uninhabited. The truth was very different.

There were thousands of people already here.

The ones whom they had encountered had given them cause to fret. These were not like the men they were used to. These men wore guns on their hips and seemed to know how to use those lethal weapons.

Caleb had heard tell of distant farmers such as themselves having their stock killed and their crops destroyed, but so far nothing bad had happened to him or his closest neighbours.

Yet during the dark nights, Caleb and his wife Bessie had heard the chilling sound of gunfire away in the distance. They had also seen flames rising into the night sky. They had experienced similar things back East, but the land was so big here and devoid of man-made structures that it somehow reinforced their feelings of total isolation.

Caleb and his fellow settlers had become careful.

Their trips into the towns for supplies were becoming more and more unpleasant. For the newly arrived people, who knew little of weapons, and the men who lived by their expertise with them, were for some reason, enemies.

Caleb had never had an enemy before in his entire life.

The thought of gaining them now could not dampen his resolve to stay in the valley, though. He would never return to the place he had come from. Not alive, anyway.

It had become a habit for several of the settlers to go into Hangman's Corner together in the hope that they would be protected by numbers. Yet ruthless killers and hired gunfighters were not so easily intimidated. Only men with guns impressed their sort.

Mere farmers only enraged them.

Each day had become more and more nerve-racking as rumours drifted within the isolated communities about the hooded riders who seemed hell-bent on driving Caleb and his kind out of the lush valley.

But Caleb Watkins had dreamt of this place for too long to be frightened by mere rumours. He had never been a violent man but would not give up his hundred acres without a fight.

Caleb knew that this was his home. He would not quit this place whatever happened.

If the hooded riders came to the Watkins farm, Caleb knew that he would try and fight them off until his last drop of blood had been drained from his body.

He would never leave the Pecos Valley alive.

Whoever the hooded riders were, they had not struck at his small farm yet. But he felt in his bones that it was only a matter of time.

For some reason to which he was not privy they wanted the settlers to return to wherever they had come from. Caleb knew that he would rather die than return to the hell that he had escaped from.

For the first time in his entire life, he had a chance of making a real future for Bessie and little Rosemary. There might be angry men here with deadly guns but the air was pure and the sky blue.

There was heat in the sun that warmed his bones and had taken the stiffness from his joints.

Whoever the hooded riders were, they could not scare a man like Caleb Watkins. He had suffered for too long in a place these riders could not even envisage.

If there was evil here and it sought him out, he would meet it head on.

Caleb had no weapons and came to learn that this was a land where they were vital. There was not enough money left to purchase even an old pistol or rifle and he was beginning to realize that without one he might not be able to protect his family or their farm.

Then he saw the dust rising in the distance as the sun was starting to set.

'Riders!' Caleb muttered under his breath.

# FIVE

The sun had set swiftly on the range and sent crimson fingers stretching out above the heads of all who dwelled beneath the slowly emerging canopy of stars. The pair of horsemen had spotted the small house made of trimmed tree-trunks an hour earlier as they guided their mounts through the brush that banked the Pecos River. It had been light then, but now the light was fading quickly. Tom Dix and Dan Shaw slowed their horses as they approached the small wooden house. A single lantern hung from the roof overhang and they could make out the silhouette of a man standing directly before its faint amber light. Both riders knew the value of caution and eased back on their reins until the horses were walking slowly enough for their observer to get a good look at them.

Dan Shaw tapped his companion's sleeve and leaned across the distance between their saddles.

'We better be darn careful, Dixie. I don't cotton to being shot off my horse by no farmer.'

'Me neither.'

'I can't make him out clearly,' Dan said, rubbing the dust from his eyes. 'Can you?'

Dix reined in and stopped his horse. His keen eyes narrowed and he stared off into the fading light at the shape of the man who was facing them. Darkness posed no problem to his experienced eyes.

'He's unarmed, Dan.'

Shaw pulled back on his own reins and looked at the man ahead of them in the small courtyard. He still could not see him clearly.

'You can actually see that he ain't carrying no scattergun or the like from here, Dixie?'

'Yep.'

Dan shrugged. 'No wonder you've always been a better shot than me.'

'It does kinda help if you can see what you aim at,' Tom Dix said, running the palm of his gloved hand along the neck of his alert mount.

They continued looking at the man who was watching them. He walked slowly towards his fence. Whoever this farmer was, he was brave, Dix thought. Anyone who squared up to a pair of well-armed strangers with only his courage as protection, deserved a lot of respect.

Tom Dix dismounted and glanced at his partner. 'You ought to get yourself some of them store-bought eyeglasses that old folks wear, Dan.'

It was an unconvinced Dan Shaw who got down from his saddle and gathered up his reins. He could not take his eyes off the eerie figure within the small farmyard.

'Are you certain that he ain't got no gun, Dixie?'

Tom Dix led his tall horse towards the man who was now almost at the small gate.

'Come on, Dan. I'll take care of you.'

Caleb Watkins rested his hands on top of the fence and inhaled deeply. Whoever these two strangers were, they were too much like the other gun-toting men he had seen at Hangman's Corner. Had his turn finally come to be intimidated?

'Who are you?' he asked.

Tom Dix touched the brim of his hat, walked up to the fence and wrapped his reins around its unpainted wood.

'The name's Tom Dix, friend.'

Caleb's eyes flashed at Dan Shaw as nervously he joined his partner before returning to Dix.

'What do you men want here?'

The retired lawman did not recognize the accent. 'My name's Dan Shaw. What they call you?'

'Caleb Watkins. This is my farm. Like I said, what do you want here?'

'Just a little water for our horses and canteens, Caleb,' Dix said in a hushed tone. 'I'm sorry if we kinda scared you turning up after sundown.'

The farmer swallowed hard. He wanted to believe the words but knew that this land bred a different sort of man than he was used to. 'Are you part of that hooded rider bunch?'

Dix leaned on the fence and stared into the

45

face. Even in the light of the moon he could tell that Caleb was serious.

'Hooded riders?' Dix repeated. 'Are you telling us that there's a gang of hooded riders roaming these ranges?'

'Yeah, hired men who have been burning the settlers out,' the farmer clarified. 'They always wait until dark before they strike and that's why you boys made me nervous.'

'We ain't part of no outlaw gang, Caleb.' Dix rested a hand on the arm of the man. The farmer turned and looked at the wrinkled face. 'I swear to you. We ain't saddle trash.'

Caleb Watkins rubbed his mouth.

'I've been expecting them to strike here. They already drove off a dozen or more settlers further north. Seeing you riding up made me think that it was my turn to have my animals killed and crops ruined.'

Dan Shaw stepped closer.

'You look like a man who could use a little help, Caleb.'

Caleb Watkins shook his head. 'I ain't got no money to pay for no help, stranger.'

'Did we ask for any money?' Dix asked as he removed his Stetson and hung it on one of his gun grips. 'Me and Dan got us enough money to tide us over for a while.'

'I don't understand. . . ?'

Dan Shaw wrapped his reins around the top of the fence and tied a secure knot. 'Me and Dixie

46

here are used to tangling with outlaws, Caleb. We can help you and your fellow settlers if you like.'

'But why?' Caleb asked. He was confused. 'Why would you want to help a total stranger?'

There was a long pause as the two riders looked at one another. It was a good question. Both horsemen knew that even they did not have an answer.

'What do you think, Dixie?'

'We ain't got nothing better to do, Dan.' Dix smiled.

Caleb Watkins heard the door of his small home open behind him and all three men looked at the scared figure of Bessie standing in the dim illumination. She was visibly shaking.

'There's nothing to worry yourself about, Bessie. These men are our friends. They've come to help us.'

'Do they want a little supper?' Bessie asked quietly.

Dix and Dan both bowed their heads respectfully.

'Thank you, ma'am,' they seemed to say together.

# SIX

Fort Liberty stood fifty miles east of the Pecos River. It had once been a vital link in the long chain of military outposts which were scattered across the sun-baked plains. But that had been when the numerous tribes of nomadic Indians had posed a continuous reminder that this land had already been occupied long before any white man had ever set foot upon it.

With the virtual destruction of the once seemingly limitless herds of buffalo, the Plains Indians had also disappeared. It had been more than ten years since any of the soldiers who manned the isolated fortress had even seen any of the once prolific warriors anywhere near the deteriorating garrison.

There had been a thousand reasons then why Fort Liberty had been a vital link in the chain of outposts which gradually brought stability to an unstable land. In the years that followed, its importance had disappeared like the buffalo and the Indians.

49

Now fewer than thirty troopers remained in the remote fort. It had been decided far away in the chambers of power that when their term of duty was over, in less than six months' time, Fort Liberty would be abandoned and left to be reclaimed by the desert.

There were few reasons for maintaining an expensive outpost in a land that was of little value any more. It had served its purpose.

Major Harry Travis was a man abandoned by his superiors. He had done everything that he had ever been called upon to do and more. He had ensured that the hostile Apache, who had once roamed this land freely, were driven off. The other tribes who had fought valiantly against his once massive force had been either defeated in battle or sent away to the swamps of distant Florida; a fate that was worse than death to a people who were unaccustomed to its totally different climate.

Travis had conquered everything except the politics which went hand in hand with command. He had never learned how to play the game his masters' way.

He had suffered from honesty. It was a fatal flaw.

For all the years that he had commanded Fort Liberty on this treacherous terrain, Travis had never been promoted or even considered for transfer to a better garrison.

Now he knew that it was all but over. It was too late.

He had given his all and now it was obvious that

nobody cared what fate awaited him or his now depleted force.

Major Harrison Travis strode along the high fortress walkway from one tower to the next and stared out at the land that he had helped to tame.

Now he knew that he had done his difficult job far too well. A man of lesser moral character would have allowed some of his enemies to elude him and the Springfield rifles of his soldiers.

If only there was still an active threat out there, he thought.

For if there were still hostile forces roaming around the territory unchecked, he and his beloved fort would still be seen to be important.

Travis chewed on the end of his pipe-stem and gazed out into the night, which was illuminated by a large moon. Yet wherever his keen eyes looked, only tumbleweed dared to move across the sand. He shook his head and sighed. The official letter that he had received more than a month earlier informed him that his services would not be required after the last day of August.

Other men in his position would have been offered desk jobs back East, but not him. He had spoken his mind too often and upset those who thought of themselves as his betters.

Travis had still more than ten years of service left in him but the army had told him in no uncertain terms that he was to take early retirement and a reduced pension.

Travis inhaled deeply and clenched his fists.

51

How could they simply discard him like an old shoe? Surely men with his record were worth more than that. It seemed not. The letter that was neatly folded up in his tunic breast-pocket had been blunt and brutal.

He was of no use to the modern army.

His day had passed.

Where were all the enemies? Had he defeated them all?

Major Travis knew that the politicians were wrong about Fort Liberty. He knew that trouble could raise its ugly head at any time. Once the fort was abandoned , it would be virtually impossible to reactivate it again. The men who made the laws were far away in a place that had never seen any of the horrors which he knew still prevailed in the West.

It might be quiet here now, he thought, but that was because he had done his job well. Once there was no army presence in the territory, it would not be long before the forces of evil returned.

Travis touched the pocket and felt the folded paper and then cursed silently. His services were not even needed elsewhere on the vast land that still boasted more than a dozen untamed Indian tribes. He had heard stories that to the north many tribes were gathering in larger numbers than had ever been seen before. The Sioux, Cheyenne and Navajo had been driven away from their hunting grounds and ancestral homes.

It was said that they were now joining forces.

Soon the combined tribes would stand their

ground and fight. Experienced soldiers such as himself knew that once again trouble was brewing, but the army was not run by soldiers. It was controlled by bookkeepers.

The disheartened officer made his way down the wooden ladder towards the men who were gathered in the large parade ground and walked toward them.

Every one of them was a seasoned veteran. Men you could trust with your life.

They too were being pensioned off before their time and would have to somehow survive on a half-pension. The broad-shouldered major strode across to the men and halted. He acknowledged the salutes and then sat down on an upturned barrel amid them.

He still had not told them the sordid truth of what their masters had planned for them. The information was still in his pocket and he could not bring himself to tell these loyal troopers that soon they would all be abandoned to their fate.

He accepted a cup of coffee and blew at the hot surface.

'When we going out on patrol again, sir?' one of the soldiers asked.

Major Travis stared through the steam.

'Tomorrow. We shall leave the fort tomorrow at dawn and ride west to the Pecos River.'

'Anything wrong, sir?' one of the men asked.

'Nothing at all, trooper,' Travis lied. 'Nothing at all.'

53

# SEVEN

A blazing sun had traced its way across the Pecos Valley and brought the roosters out from their hiding-places. A new day had dawned on the unsettled land. But this was one that would be remembered long after the sun had set again. One that would bring more bloodshed to the vast range than any other day had done before it.

Yet on the small Watkins homestead, as well as its neighbours, there was no hint as to what was looming only hours away.

Soon there would be acrid gunsmoke hanging on the air.

Unknown to the innocent, the fuse had already been lit.

Tom Dix awoke first and stared around the interior of the crude tool-shack. Dix looked across at his still-snoring friend and smiled. The hay beneath their bedrolls had been a luxury to men who had slept on the hard sun-baked range for the past few weeks.

The screeching rooster had not been hatched that could wake Dan Shaw.

Dix yawned and heard the sound of hens moving around the small fenced yard. The aroma of breakfast being cooked inside the small house drifted into the three-walled shack.

He raised himself up on his elbows and rubbed the sleep from his eyes. The tired eyes glanced again at his friend a few feet away from him, sleeping peacefully. Dan's bones had been stiffening up since they had started out on the trail together. Dix knew that the retired lawman had spent nearly all his life sleeping in a real bed. The past six months or so had taken its toll on Dan far more than on him. Dix had survived twelve years sleeping on a prison cot and compared with that, everything else was comfortable.

Even a hard prairie floor was softer than a prison cot. The once famed gunfighter ran his fingers through his grey hair and watched the hay falling before his eyes through the rays of morning sun.

Then suddenly he saw her.

She was no more than three feet tall and had long, dark, wavy hair and a smile that could melt ice. Dix had heard Caleb and Bessie speak of their daughter over supper but she had been asleep in her small cot.

The little girl was looking straight at him. Dix wondered how long she had been standing there silently. She had hold of the frayed hem of her nightdress and held it to her mouth, as all little girls do. Dix returned the smile and sat upright.

'Howdy, young 'un.'

She continued smiling but said nothing.

'What's your name?' Dix asked.

'Rosemary.'

'That's a darn pretty name.'

'Who are you?'

'My name's Tom Dix but folks kinda call me Dixie.'

'Why?'

'I'm not sure.'

'Dixie is a girl's name,' Rosemary informed the smiling man as he managed to get to his feet.

'I reckon you're right, Rosemary.'

Her little finger pointed at his snoring companion.

'Who is that?'

'My friend. His name's Dan.'

'Is he old like you?'

Dix grinned. 'Nobody is as old as me, honey.'

'Is he your son?'

'Nope. He's just a friend.'

Then the sound of Bessie's voice drifted through the air and alerted the child that her breakfast was ready. The girl began to move and then glanced up at the man.

'I like you, Dixie.'

Before Dix could respond, she had run across the yard and entered the small house. Dix grinned.

'I like you as well, Rosemary.'

'Who you talking to, Dixie?' Dan Shaw asked as he began rising from the hay. 'There ain't nobody here. You weren't talking to them hens, was you?'

Tom Dix shook his head, walked across to his boots and picked them up.

'I was talking to the little girl.'

Dan exhaled and looked around the shack.

'Where is she?'

'She headed off for breakfast,' Dix said, pulling the first of his boots on.

Dan sniffed at the air.

'Can you smell fried ham, Dixie?'

'Yep.'

'I'd give a silver dollar for a plate of fried ham.'

Dix pulled the second boot on and then pointed towards the house. Dan looked up and saw the small child returning to the shack.

'Momma said you can have breakfast with us.'

Before either man could reply, the small child had run back to the house.

'These folks ain't got much but they're willing to share it with the likes of us.' Dix sighed.

'Reckon we ought to ride to the nearest town and buy them some provisions,' Dan said as he found his own boots amid the hay.

'After breakfast, partner.'

'We might find out who those hooded riders are,' Dan added.

Tom Dix started walking towards the house and the aroma of cooking. With every stride he thought about the words of his friend. Who were the hooded riders and what did they want with these innocent people?

# EIGHT

Pecos City was little more than a sprawling array of small adobe structures whose name exaggerated its importance. It had been the first of the three towns which had sprung up quickly to satisfy the wants and needs of the hundreds of badmen who had discovered the fertile ranges. Another town named Wildcat had soon followed and then, finally, Hangman's Corner.

Wildcat lay almost abandoned far to the western fringes of the valley whilst Pecos City only survived due to its close proximity to a couple of the notorious ranches.

Few gunhands ventured into the boundaries of Pecos City any longer, preferring the larger more prosperous Hangman's Corner further to the south. The younger town had more saloons and brothels, but its prices were high.

Pecos City was, however, the best place for men to spend their ill-gotten gains, for prices did not rise and fall like the temperature in the poorer town.

The couple of ranchers who had built their large houses close to the the self-proclaimed city seldom drifted down to Hangman's Corner because they knew that this was Cal Harrigan's town. Like the valley itself, he ruled there like a self-anointed king.

His word was law.

His guns enforced that law.

But Pecos City had a far more important value to those who knew of it and its neighbour. It was a place where certain types of men could hide in safety. Nobody asked questions in Pecos City. Few strangers ever rode into Pecos City. Those who did, only did so for a very good reason.

Men could remain virtually untroubled here.

Men who, although very like the rest of the vermin who dwelled in the valley, and who lived by their gun skills, were cut from a very different cloth.

They were not mere gunhands.

They were deadly hired assassins who roamed the West like shadows. Men whose names were well known and yet few could claim ever to have set eyes upon them.

These faceless creatures did other men's bidding. They were the men who killed for an agreed price. They would kill anyone if their fee was forthcoming. No man, woman or even child was safe once they had been paid their blood-money.

They were even more evil than those who

already dwelled on the vast ranges of the Pecos Valley. For the hired gunslingers who rode with the rich ranchers were simply men who were experts with their shooting irons. They were simply protection for the rich outlaw cattlemen who paid them.

The hired assassins were known by another name.

They were called the shootists.

No other name put fear into the hearts of even hardened gunfighters like that of the shootist. For these rare riders were no ordinary gunmen.

The shootists were willing to kill anyone by any means. They would shoot their target in the back or even set fire to an entire building to earn their fee. Yet this did not mean that they could not use their weaponry.

They were experts with their guns and rifles if called upon to use them.

The shootists were few in number, but no less terrifying for that.

Men such as these took no prisoners.

Their business was death.

They killed in the same way that most men breathe. Without a second thought. To them it was natural.

Yet they were not hired on the mere whims of those with simple grudges, seeking to exact vengeance. They were far too dangerous for that. The shootist was a killing machine who would turn on those who hired their skills if they did not get everything they wanted.

To hire a shootist was to grab a rattler by its tail. It could turn, coil and strike without warning.

Matt Blair was a shootist.

He had arrived at Pecos City nearly ten days earlier and remained within the confines of the small hotel room he had paid for thirty days in advance. He sought no company to occupy his time whilst he was waiting. For he knew how to wait better than most men.

No one had set eyes upon the notorious hired gun since he had first ridden in. That was the way he liked it. His was a lonely trade and it was far better for him never to associate with anyone whom he might one day be called upon to kill. Shootists had no friends. They preferred it that way. It made killing simpler and neater for all concerned.

Matt Blair ate in his room and only ventured out to answer the call of nature.

Even then he was like a phantom, unseen by any of the hotel staff.

Blair had been sent a fat retainer just to come to Pecos City and wait for instructions.

When the knock came at his hotel door, he glanced at his gold hunter watch that rested on the dresser. It was not quite seven in the morning and too early for breakfast.

The shootist rose from his bed and pulled both his lethal Colts from their holsters. He cocked their hammers until they locked and then walked towards the unpainted door.

'Who is it?'

'Harrigan!'

# NINE

It was an unusually cautious Cal Harrigan who entered the stuffy hotel room alone. It was the first time he had been without his army of hired gunhands for twenty years. He had little knowledge of fear but sweat began to trail down his face from his thinning hair. Matt Blair made him nervous. Harrigan held on to his large ten-gallon hat in his gloved hands and walked past the tall thin man.

The air within the room stank of stale cigar smoke, but it was not that which made Harrigan feel himself sinking in a pool of his own sweat.

Harrigan turned and looked hard at the shootist and wondered if it had been such a smart idea sending for him. There was a cruelty in the face of Matt Blair that the rancher had never seen before.

It frightened him.

The two men continued to stare silently at one another as if waiting for the other to crack. They were both disappointed.

Neither showed any outward sign of emotion as they weighed each other up. Harrigan moved to the window and tried vainly to open it.

'It don't open, Harrigan,' Matt Blair announced as he sat on the edge of his bed and slid his pair of guns back into their holsters.

'How can you stand it in here? It's like an inferno.' The rancher lifted the tails of his bandanna off his shirt front, raised them, wiped the beads of sweat from his eyes and then turned back to face the shootist.

'I like it hot,' the stony voice snapped.

'But this is unbearable.' Harrigan removed his coat and sighed heavily. He was about to say more when the deadly man spoke again in a hushed tone.

'I said I like the heat. It keeps me lean.'

'I take it ya don't cotton to fresh air either.'

'There ain't no fresh air in Pecos City, Harrigan,' Matt Blair said. He placed a long thin cigar between his teeth and neatly bit off the end. 'This place stinks of horses and cattle. Nope, I don't cotton to that sort of fresh air.'

Harrigan watched Blair spit the small tobacco tip on the floor. There must have been fifty other such cigar tips covering the floor near the corner. Blair had obviously been here a lot longer than he had thought. He wondered why. Why would he have arrived so much earlier than their agreed appointment date?

The rancher cleared his throat nervously and

asked: 'Was the price agreeable?'

'I'm here ain't I?' Blair replied bluntly.

The rancher nodded and walked around the small sweltering room. He had never felt as nervous as he did now in the presence of this renowned killer.

'Yep. You're here OK.'

'The details were a little vague though.' Blair struck a match. He lifted the flame to the end of the long cigar and sucked. Smoke swirled around his narrowed features as his eyes trailed Harrigan around the room. 'I like to know who I'm meant to kill so that I can prepare things.'

'There's only so much you can put in a letter, Blair.'

'Mr Blair, Harrigan,' the shootist corrected sharply. 'You will show me the respect that I deserve. OK?'

Harrigan's eyes narrowed. Nobody had dared speak to him like that in more than twenty years. He felt his temper rise swiftly until he focused on the emotionless face watching him. Suddenly Harrigan knew how this man's victims must have felt a split second before Blair destroyed them.

'I'm sorry, Mr Blair.' Harrigan heard himself say. 'I forgot my manners.'

Matt Blair nodded and inhaled on the cigar. He allowed the smoke to filter through his teeth slowly. It was obvious that this man liked his job. He enjoyed killing and it showed in his every slightest expression.

'Who exactly am I meant to kill?' Blair asked. 'I want a name and details of where this *hombre* holds out.'

The question was blunt and accurate. The rancher swallowed hard and stopped pacing. He looked down on the seated man and tried to remember that this was not a man to make angry.

'It ain't just one man that I need killed.'

Matt Blair's eyes flashed through the smoke at Harrigan.

'I don't like the sound of this, Harrigan.'

Harrigan wiped the sweat off his upper lip. 'I need you to organize the total destruction of the settlers who have set up their homesteads along the eastern fringes of my valley.'

Blair eyebrows slowly rose.

'You made me think that this was a straightforward execution, Harrigan. Now you start telling me something different. I don't like it.'

The rancher tried to calm the shootist. 'I have a real big problem here that needs your expertise, Mr Blair.'

'This will cost you a lot more than we agreed, Harrigan.'

The rancher's face went pale.

'We had a deal.'

'For one execution.' Blair smiled as he sucked the end of the long cigar.

'But I thought that . . .'

'One execution.' Blair's voice was raised just

loud enough to snuff out the rancher's protest. 'You seem to be talking about killing hundreds of men, women and children. That'll cost a darn sight more than the fee we agreed. If you argue with me over this point, I shall surely kill you here and now.'

Cal Harrigan turned away from the shootist and moved back to the window. His hand rubbed at the grime until he was able to look down into the street. He watched his hired men standing next to their horses.

He knew that none of them had an ounce of Blair's acrid blood running through their veins. They would kill, but not like this notorious man.

'I have a lot of men outside this hotel, Mr Blair. Men that would not like you killing me,' Harrigan said quietly.

'They will not give a damn,' Blair said coldly. 'Once the man who pays their salary is dead, they will just ride away and seek another paymaster. I've seen it a dozen times. Loyalty does not go further than the undertaker's parlour.'

Cal Harrigan looked at the slight smile on the shootist's face. It was the smile of someone who knew exactly what he was talking about. 'You'd kill me?'

Blair nodded. 'Yep. I'd kill you and anyone else who makes the mistake of trying to trick me.'

'You misunderstand my motives. I ain't been trying to trick anybody. All I want you to do for me is to plan the whole thing,' Harrigan said. 'I want

71

you to work out all the details. Then my boys will do as you order.'

'How much will this job pay, Harrigan?' Blair blew out a long line of grey smoke at the floor.

The rancher brooded. 'I'll add an extra five thousand dollars to the original fee.'

There was a chilling silence as both men stood their ground. Yet there would be only one winner in this battle of wits. The handsome pair of lethal pistols in Matt Blair's holsters had already won the argument. It only remained for Harrigan to acknowledge that fact.

'Make that ten thousand dollars and you've got yourself a deal.' Matt Blair smiled at the man before him. Both knew that if Harrigan disagreed, he would die in the small hot hotel room.

Harrigan spun on his heels and was about to curse when he saw the cold eyes fixed on him. It was as if every ounce of his courage had been sucked from his body.

'Ten thousand more?'

The shootist looked straight into the eyes of the rancher and defied him to object. 'Yeah.'

Harrigan swallowed his pride and lowered his chin until it touched his chest.

'Agreed.'

# TEN

Tom Dix had been working hard on the weathered old wagon since eating breakfast at the table of Caleb and Bessie Watkins. For more than an hour he had toiled like a man half his age whilst everyone looked on. But all offers of help had been refused. This was a job that the man wanted to do all by himself. As if he were paying for the food he had eaten.

The prairie schooner had not been used since Caleb Watkins and his small family had arrived in the Pecos Valley over eight weeks earlier. It had been stripped of all the trimmings it had required to transport the small family over a thousand miles of treacherous land. Now it would be adapted into a vehicle that Caleb could use.

It had taken the knowledgeable wits of the man who had started his working life as a cowboy to get the wagon into shape. Dix knew how and seemed obsessed with doing this for their hosts. A little grease on the axle rods and wheel hubs and the

73

vehicle was as good as new.

'You sure you don't want me to help you, Dixie?' Dan shouted across the yard.

'What do you know about wagons?' Dix replied.

The wagon sorted out, its team had been a different matter. The four mules had grazed in a fenced-off section of the homestead until Tom Dix led two of the creatures out and harnessed them in the long wooden traces.

It had taken half an hour to persuade the skittish, stubborn animals that their services were once again required, but Dix had somehow succeeded in the end.

Once hitched up, the mules suddenly seemed eager to get back to work.

Caleb watched as the silver-haired Dix worked silently, going about his chores of feeding their chickens and milking the swollen cow.

He had said nothing but the look upon his face showed his gratitude.

Dan Shaw had tried to assist his partner but his efforts were rejected. Shaw sat on the doorstep next to the talkative Rosemary Watkins for what seemed an eternity, feeling guilty that he seemed to be the only adult with nothing to do.

Finally Tom Dix was satisfied with his efforts and strode back to his friend.

'You look darned pleased with yourself, Dixie,' Dan commented.

'I enjoyed doing that.' Dix smiled, accepting a ladle of water. He downed it quickly. 'Must be twenty years since I hitched up a team to a wagon.'

'But why did you do it?' Dan asked.

'These folks need a wagon to get themselves and supplies to and from town.' Dix sighed.

'Guess so.' Dan nodded.

'I'm going to the town they call Hangman's Corner to get some provisions for these folks right now,' Dix announced.

'I'm going along with you.'

Dix held his friend's elbow and pulled him to his feet. The two faces were nose to nose.

'I don't think that would be too smart, Dan.'

Dan Shaw's expression altered.

'What ya mean?'

'I figured that I'd take Caleb with me and leave you here to protect the woman and the girl,' Dix whispered.

'You figure that there might be trouble here, Dixie?'

'There might be.'

Dan nodded.

'OK. I'll look after these females.'

Dix smiled.

'And they couldn't be in safer hands.'

# ELEVEN

Death stalked the barren wastes that led to the wide Pecos river and the infamous land which lay beyond its western shoreline. The riders had followed the straight-backed cavalry major since dawn had beckoned another blisteringly hot new day. The men were, as always, well prepared. Major Travis had ensured that they had enough pack-animals to carry any equipment, provisions and water the trek might require.

During all the years that Travis had guided his troops over the hot merciless landscape, they had never been caught lacking anything that might mean the difference between life and death.

Travis believed that it was always wiser to have too much equipment with you, even on a routine mission, than not enough.

The officer was still haunted by the memories of one of his first scouting trips when he had been stationed far to the north at Fort Grant. He had seen what could happen when you rode into the jaws of the unexpected and came face to face with a superior force. It had been the Cheyenne back then.

His commanding officer had seen eighty men killed and what was left of his cavalry barely capable of limping back to their garrison. In all the years that Travis had been stationed at Fort Liberty, he had never once made the same mistake that he had seen his complacent superiors make that fateful day.

Even if he knew that there were no enemies out there in the maze of tall cactus and white-hot sand, he still prepared as if he were going into battle. He had vowed that he would never watch his men killed because of his own arrogance.

He took nothing for granted, not even the sun that burned through his tunic. He knew that things could alter in the blink of an eye and you had to be ready for that change. He had always been ready.

Travis gripped his reins tightly in his gloved hands and looked over his shoulder at the troopers who rode slowly behind his black gelded charger. There were just twenty-four men riding two abreast across the seemingly lifeless ground between the tall Judas trees and the gruesome cactus. To the rear of the silent procession, four pack-horses followed.

The twenty-five riders had left a skeleton crew back at Fort Liberty to await their return with a well-deserved hot supper. The cavalry patrol had been in the saddle for more than two hours, heading due west. They had maintained an even pace that they knew would not make their horses lather up.

This was not a land in which to allow one's precious horses to get too tired. The tiny brain of the average cavalry mount could boil inside its skull beneath the ferocious sun.

Travis raised his right hand and brought his men to a stop. He dismounted quickly and stood looking at the shimmering water that lay less than a mile ahead of them through the dry brush.

Sergeant Olaf Svenson walked up to the thoughtful officer and cleared his throat. He waited for the eyes of his superior to glance in his direction before speaking.

'Aye, it's a grand sight, Major Travis. All that lovely water just flowing along like it's done since God first created this place.' Svenson sighed.

Travis looked back at the large man who towered above him.

'What?'

'I was just saying how pretty the river looks, sir.' Svenson shrugged. 'It is a grand vision, ain't it?'

Major Travis pulled his trusty pipe out from his hip pocket and placed the yellow stem between his teeth.

'When you start getting poetic with me, I know something's wrong, Sergeant. What's wrong?'

The wide-shouldered enlisted man shrugged and leaned over in a vain attempt to reduce the difference in their respective heights.

'Me and the little boys was wondering if we will be heading back to Fort Liberty after we lets the nags fill their bellies with water?'

Major Travis knew that this was probably one of their last patrols and yet there was something eating at his craw. He felt something in his experienced bones that he could neither explain or understand.

'You figure that we are wasting our time, Sergeant?' Travis reached behind him and grabbed at the reins hanging from his mount's bridle. He began to walk the horse and could hear his men all doing the same.

'Well to put it bluntly, sir, yes. I do think that we are getting our hides burned off for no real reason.' Olaf Svenson walked with his own horse trailing behind his wide rump like a faithful hound.

Travis glanced across the distance between them.

'You ever had yourself a feeling that you cannot explain, Sergeant Svenson?'

The large sergeant rubbed his whiskers and pushed out his lower lip in considered thought. He studied the shorter man who always looked immaculate, even when covered in trail dust. He knew that there was something troubling Harry Travis.

'What do you mean, sir?'

The twenty-five men all walked their horses

closer and closer to the crystal-clear river.

'I cannot explain it. There is something making me want to lead you men across the river into the Pecos Valley.' Travis knew that his words would stun the huge man walking beside him.

They did.

Svenson rubbed the dust from his face with the palm of his large hand and then shook his head in disbelief at what he had just heard the normally logical officer say.

'But we never ride over the river into the Pecos Valley, sir,' he protested. 'There ain't no law over there. That's an untamed land filled with outlaws and riff-raff. They'd shoot us off the backs of our horses before we even reached the heart of the place.'

Travis nodded to every word that fell from the lips of his troubled companion. He looked back at the troopers who followed them loyally towards the river. Then he moved closer to Svenson. He did not want the men to overhear anything that passed between them.

'The government has opened that land up to settlers, Olaf.'

The statement stunned the sergeant.

'What? Are they loco?'

Travis nodded. 'Reckon they must be.'

'They can't send innocent farmers into the Pecos Valley and hope that they survive long enough to see their first crops reach harvesting time,' Svenson growled as he kept pace with the more spry officer.

'They've already done it.'

Olaf Svenson drew in his barrel belly and looked in horror at the grim-faced Travis.

'They've already sent people in there?'

'Yep. I heard that more than a hundred wagons have crossed over into the Pecos Valley during the past six months.' The major's eyes flashed at the enlisted man as if trying to see whether there were any answers hidden inside the wise head.

Svenson pulled his battered hat from his head and ran his sleeve across his sweat-soaked temple.

'But we ain't seen no wagons passing Fort Liberty.' Svenson was confused. 'Are you certain about these settlers, sir?'

'Dead certain. We have not seen the wagons because they have been heading twenty miles further north into the so-called new territory.' Major Travis chewed on the pipe stem and continued marching toward the fast-flowing water before them. 'I only know about it because it was mentioned in dispatches.'

'But I would have thought that they'd have wanted a military escort, sir.' Svenson was confused.

'That's what has been worrying me,' Travis said honestly. 'God knows, these farmers have required an escort, but again my hands have been tied. The authorities have been trying to make out that it is merely another unoccupied land across the Pecos river just waiting to be civilized. I imagine that they think that if we had escorted the settlers into that place, it might have caused people to ask awkward questions. Questions that have no answers.'

Travis and the loyal sergeant stopped at the water's edge and allowed their mounts to drop their long necks and drink freely from the cool flowing river. The rest of their patrol caught up and did the same.

The grim face of the sergeant was grey as they both released their grips on their reins and walked away from the scene.

The major glanced up at the blindingly hot sun and then found a place where he could sit. The large man managed to get down on the soft sand beside him and they said nothing whilst they watched the troopers watering the horses and filling their canteens. It was a few hours before noon and the sun still had a long time to do its worst for anyone who ventured out beneath its hot rays.

At last Olaf Svenson broke the silence between the two.

'Do you reckon that we are needed over there, sir?'

Travis shrugged.

'I think that we might be, but who knows? I hope that I'm just being stupid.'

Svenson dropped his hat on the crown of his head and squinted out at the landscape beyond the wide river. It was a deceptive place that gave no hint as to what lay beyond the dried brush in the unseen valley.

'There ain't no law over there. If we ride across

that river we'll be doing so without a leg to stand
on, sir. The army would wash their hands of us
once they found out.'

'I know that, Olaf. But I just feel that something's wrong. If I'm incorrect, nothing is lost. We
just turn around and head back over here and on
to Fort Liberty.'

'But if'n you happen to be right?' The sergeant
bit his lip and watched as his superior removed his
white gauntlets and pulled out his tobacco pouch.
The nimble fingers filled the pipe bowl as the
man's eyes searched the horizon over the river for
clues.

'We'll have to fight,' Travis said. He placed the
pipe into his mouth and chewed on the yellow
stem.

'I always liked a good fight.' Svenson struck a
match, placed it above the pipe bowl and watched
as the major sucked its flame into it. He removed
the pipe from his lips and offered it to the
sergeant.

'Want a smoke?'

Olaf smiled, took the pipe in his big hand and
inhaled on the stem of the pipe. The big man
coughed and then returned it to Travis.

'You ought to use tobacco, sir. That tumbleweed
has a darn bad taste.'

Travis accepted the pipe and placed it back
between his teeth.

'If you don't want to follow me over there, Olaf,
I'll understand.'

'I'll tell the little boys that we are going for a ride over the river.'

Travis nodded.

'Make sure that they're fully armed, Olaf. I want their rifles primed and ready for action. We might not have a chance to give many offers if things get ugly.'

The big man sighed heavily.

'And there was me thinking that this was going to be just another of them days when nothing interesting happens.'

Travis watched Svenson rise to his feet.

'Let's pray that you are right.'

# TWELVE

Wild Bill Hickok stared across the card-table at the three men who had managed to remain in the marathon poker game with him for the last twelve hours. They were all looking the worse for wear as they held on to their hands of cards.

Hickok flicked the ash from the end of his cigar and placed it in the full ashtray. He picked up the five cards that were spread out before him and then stared at the three queens and a pair of nines.

He had been losing heavily for most of the evening and had only started getting good cards as the sun had finally risen and announced a new day. Hickok looked up at the wall clock and inhaled deeply. It was still only a few minutes before nine.

This had to be the last hand.

Nearly every cent that the gamblers had played for during the night was piled high in the centre of the table on the green baize. Each of the players had only a few dollars resting beside his hand.

They all knew that there would be only one winner.

'You ready to call?' A man named Arlo Green asked from where he was sitting directly opposite Hickok.

'We had better all place our cards on the table, boys,' Wild Bill said in a hushed tone. 'I don't reckon none of us wants to start taking IOUs.'

The players all placed their cards down carefully. It was obvious that a lot of bluffing had been going on during this last game of the session. Hickok looked at the men's cards. Only Arlo Green besides himself had a good hand.

The trouble was, it was too good.

'Four kings.' Green smiled as he stared at the full house of Wild Bill Hickok.

'That's a mighty good hand, Green,' the man with the long flowing hair said as his fingers toyed with the cards before him.

Arlo Green reached out his arms as the other players rose and walked silently out of the gaming hall. He began to rake the coins, gambling-chips and paper money towards him.

'No hard feelings, Wild Bill?' Green asked as he looked up at the emotionless features before him across the table. 'Somebody has to win and somebody has to lose. That's poker.'

'Nope. That's cheating, Green.' The words cut through the cigar-smoke-filled air and hit the gambler straight between his eyes. He stopped hauling the massive pot and leaned back in his hardback chair. He tried to smile at James Butler Hickok but found it impossible.

'Did I hear right? Did you just accuse me of cheating?'

Hickok lifted his cigar from the ash tray, placed it between his teeth and nodded slowly. His stare was like that of a haunting spectre. There was a fury in the hooded eyes which drilled into the soul of the other man.

'You heard me right, Green,' he confirmed.

'I don't like being called a cheat, Hickok.'

'Then maybe you should not cheat so obviously.' Wild Bill sat upright in his chair and allowed the two gun grips to jut out from his waist. 'Did you think that I was getting so tired that I'd not notice you pulling them kings out of your vest?'

Arlo Green's face went red.

'I never did that. You are a damn liar.'

Hickok tilted his head and smiled.

'I threw a king away when I was chasing another queen, Green.'

The face of the man opposite Hickok suddenly looked troubled.

'You threw a king away?'

Wild Bill rose slowly to his full height and towered over the table.

'You gonna admit that you cheated or are you ready to die, Green?'

'You trying to frighten me?' Green snarled.

'Nope. Just letting you know that there ain't any other choices.' Wild Bill stared straight at the man.

He knew that this card player was about to make his biggest gamble.

Arlo Green pushed the chair from beneath him and jumped to his feet. His hands went for the six-shot Remington he had concealed in his deep frock-coat pocket. His hand found the gun and pulled it out. Green's thumb pulled back the hammer as he levelled the deadly weapon at the tall figure.

Wild Bill Hickok's right hand moved faster than it had ever done before. Within a split second, he had drawn and aimed and fired. The blast that came from Hickok's pistol echoed around the gambling hall. The shot hit Green dead-centre and lifted the man off his feet. Hickok watched Arlo Green flying backwards with a gaping hole in his chest. Blood trailed through the air after him. The body landed on the floorboards and seemed to skid across the highly polished floor until it collided with a pile of stacked chairs. They crashed around the limp body.

Don Harper, the owner of the hall, looked up from his coffee and shook his head before returning his attention to his newspaper.

There was a silence after the sound of the lethal shot faded in the two men's ears.

Wild Bill Hickok picked up his winnings and then stuffed the mixture of coins and paper money into his pockets before sliding the pistol back into its holster. He strode slowly across the long empty room and glanced at the dead gambler who had made his last mistake.

Without a moment's hesitation, he continued on to the table and the man who was reading his newspaper.

'I left the gambling chips on the table,' Hickok said. 'There ought to be enough there to bury him.'

The man looked up at Hickok.

'Thanks, Wild Bill. It was only a matter of time before somebody figured out why he won so many games.'

'I gave him the option of admitting the truth.'

Harper sighed. 'Men like Arlo can't admit that, even to themselves, Wild Bill.'

'Sorry about the mess.'

'The cleaners will be here in a little while. They're used to finding bodies and mopping up blood.'

James Butler Hickok nodded. He walked towards the staircase and made his way down to the bright street. He paused and stared up and down the quiet street as his teeth gripped the cigar. Then he saw the wagon rolling towards him with two men on the high driver's seat. He recognized one of the men.

'Dixie?' he said under his breath. 'What the hell are you doing here?'

91

# THIRTEEN

Caleb Watkins steered the wagon along the quiet main street of Hangman's Corner towards the hardware store which stood beside the livery stables at the far end. The man who sat beside him watched the boardwalks like a hawk floating on a high thermal, seeking out its prey.

Tom Dix had removed the safety loops from his gun hammers long before they had rolled into the town. He was ready for anything that this notorious place might throw at him and his travelling companion, but not the unexpected sight of an old friend.

Dix had spotted the unmistakable figure of James Butler Hickok leaning on a wooden upright outside the Buckshot Gambling Hall as the vehicle rolled past the brightly coloured building. It was questionable which of them was the more surprised.

The slight bow and touch of the hat-brim which came from the smiling Hickok only confirmed to Dix that he was not imagining things.

Caleb pushed his foot down on the brake pole, hauled back on the heavy reins and stopped the pair of mules outside the hardware store. Dix climbed down and stood in the street watching the figure striding purposefully towards them.

'Who the hell is that, Dixie?' Caleb asked as he wrapped the reins around the brake pole.

'That, my friend, is none other than James Butler Hickok,' Dix said as the farmer climbed down from the high driver seat and stood on the boardwalk.

'Hickok?'

'Wild Bill Hickok.' Dix beamed.

'You know him?' Caleb asked as the storekeeper came out to greet his customers.

'Yep. I'm proud to say that me and that gent are the best of friends.'

There was a majesty in the way the tall man walked. He seemed to float across the ground as he closed in on the pair of new arrivals.

'He sure knows how to dress,' Caleb said, looking at the black knee-high boots that the gambler sported and the long tailored frock-coat which only a man of Hickok's height could wear. 'I never seen a man with hair that long, except for Buffalo Bill.'

Dix turned and glanced at the farmer.

'You've met Buffalo Bill?'

Caleb shrugged.

'Not really. I went to one of his shows when it was in the big city back East.'

Tom Dix returned his attention to the elegant figure of Hickok who was now almost upon him.

'You sure are a sight for sore eyes, Wild Bill.'

Hickok made a slight bow and then nodded.

'And you look awful as usual, Dixie.'

The two shook hands before Dix introduced Caleb to the famous gunfighting law officer.

'Pleased to meet you, Caleb,' Hickok said, stepping up on to the boardwalk and staring around the still sleeping town. 'I think you've chosen a good time of day to visit this town. Most of the backshooters are still asleep.'

Tom Dix stepped closer to the tall man.

'So you know about the trouble that's brewing, Bill.'

'I'm many things, but I'm not deaf, Dixie.' Hickok walked with the men towards the large open doorway of the hardware store and paused. 'I've heard a lot of things since my arrival. These men are fixing to send folks like Caleb here packing.'

There was a concern in the voice of Hickok that Dix had not heard for a long time. The man who seemed to care for nothing except playing cards was really troubled by the rumours which he had overheard during his long night at the poker tables. He had always tried to fight for the underdog even if he did it in a flamboyant way.

'Have you heard anything about hooded riders?' Dix asked as Caleb entered the store.

Hickok's eyebrows rose.

'Hooded riders? No, I would have remembered that.'

Tom Dix handed some money to the store-keeper and whispered into the man's ear. Then he moved back to the side of the tall thoughtful figure who was chewing on the end of his cigar.

'I thought that you were headed to Deadwood, Bill. How did you end up here?'

'I was headed for Deadwood, but thought that I'd try my luck at the card-tables here first.' Hickok ran a finger over his moustache and then leaned against a wooden upright. His hooded eyes stared around the streets which were starting to come to life.

'I wondered why you were up so early,' Dix remarked.

'It's not early, Dixie. This is very, very late.' Wild Bill sighed. 'I could sure use some supper right about now.'

Dix could sense his friend was worried even though he tried to conceal it.

'Spit it out, Wild Bill. What's eating at you?'

Hickok inhaled deeply on the cigar and then looked at Dix harder than he had ever done before. 'If I were you, Dixie, I'd get out of town fast. Your friend will attract the scum out of the gutters once the day gets a little older. This entire territory is like a stick of dynamite with the fuse half-burned down. I guess I just don't want you to get yourself tangled up in the middle of a war.'

Dix nodded.

'I'm already tangled up in it, Bill. Me and Dan are staying at Caleb's homestead and we ain't gonna leave them to fight off these varmints alone.'

Wild Bill smiled.

'Then I reckon I'll have to stick around just to repay my debt to you.'

'What debt?'

'You've saved my bacon a couple of times, Dixie,' Hickok said as he checked his pocket watch. 'I'll have to repay that when the time is right.'

Tom Dix smiled. 'Once we load up the wagon with canned goods, we'll be out of here.'

Wild Bill Hickok tossed his cigar away and then stepped down on to the street. He paused just long enough to glance over his shoulder into his friend's eyes.

'Be careful, Dixie. This town is about as bad as they get.'

Tom Dix watched as the tall man strode across the street and entered a small café. He knew that James Butler Hickok did not offer advice often and when he did, it was wise to heed it.

Hangman's Corner was just about as bad as any town could get, just as his friend had claimed. Dix could smell the evil in the air.

# FOURTEEN

Matt Blair looped his reins around the hitching rail outside Cal Harrigan's large house and kicked at the dry dusty ground. What was going through his mind none of the other riders could imagine. For the entire journey since leaving Pecos City he had said nothing.

Blair watched as the rancher and his men dismounted all around him. The sound of thundering hoofs echoed around the buildings, causing the shootist to turn and gaze out into the shimmering heat. He saw other riders closing in on the courtyard. At least thirty well armed men.

'Who the hell are they, Harrigan?' Blair asked.

'These are the other ranchers and their crews,' Harrigan replied nervously.

'How many men do we have in total?'

The rancher shrugged. 'I ain't sure. Maybe fifty or better.'

'Good.' Blair walked through the gunmen up to the large door of the ranch house, kicked it open

99

and entered. 'C'mon boys, let's get ourselves a drink of Harrigan's liquor.'

The men looked at Harrigan, wondering if they ought to obey the orders of this strange man.

Harrigan gritted his teeth and gave permission for everyone to follow the shootist into his home.

He then turned and watched as the other ranchers and their hired gunmen rode under the large sign fifty yards away from the array of buildings. The riders all drew in their reins and dismounted quickly.

Matt Blair came to the doorway and waved his arms at the riders, then walked back into the house.

'C'mon, boys. Join the party,' he called out over his shoulder.

Enos White dropped to the ground from his grey mare and marched up to Harrigan. White was a man who controlled almost as many steers on the vast range as Harrigan himself. He was also a man who did not like trouble. The sight of the shootist calling the shots made him even more nervous than taking part in the hooded-rider raids.

'Is that Matt Blair the shootist, Cal?' Enos White asked.

'Yep. That's the famous Matt Blair,' Harrigan acknowledged.

'Are you plumb loco?' White grabbed the arm of the narrow-eyed rancher. 'You hired a shootist?'

Harrigan began to inhale deeply.

'I'm starting to regret that, Enos.'

'He's deadly. None of us is safe around a man like Blair.'

'I'm beginning to realize that, Enos.' Harrigan turned to watch their men entering his home. He knew that Matt Blair was already taking over and it worried him. Where would it stop?

'He's crazy. Everybody knows that he's crazy.' White felt sweat running down his spine beneath his thick shirt. 'What possessed you to hire a shootist? He'll kill us all if the mood takes him.'

Cal Harrigan moved slowly past the horses towards the open doorway. It was like approaching a gallows.

'It seemed like a good idea at the time. I figured that if we wanted to get rid of them settlers, we needed someone who was used to killing people, but as soon as I met him up at Pecos City, I knew that I'd bitten off more than I could chew.'

'I heard tell that he killed Johnny Ringo in Tombstone,' White whispered in to the ear of the troubled Harrigan.

'I wouldn't be surprised. He's already threatened to kill me.'

Enos White's face went pale. 'Shootists are always trouble but I've heard that Matt Blair is the worst of a bad bunch. I seen his picture on the front page of a newspaper in Dodge. He had killed an entire outlaw gang single handed.'

Harrigan shook his head angrily. 'If I'd known that, I'd have shied away from hiring him in the first place. Now it looks like we have to try and make the best of it.'

'But can we keep him under control?'

Matt Blair came from the shadows of the house and glared at the two men. There was death in his eyes. He curled his finger at them and then walked back into the noisy house.

'Get your hides inside here. I have some plans to discuss with you critters,' Blair shouted.

'Well?' White pressed for an answer.

Harrigan glanced at White before leading his fellow rancher through the doorway.

'I got me a feeling that nobody can, Enos.'

# FIFTEEN

Joe Conway led his two fellow Harrigan gunmen from the saloon and stood watching the provisions being loaded up on to the back of the wagon by Tom Dix and Caleb Watkins. For a moment he was taken aback.

'Well just look over yonder, boys. What do you see?'

'Dirt farmers,' Sam Cole said beside the brooding Conway as they walked out beneath the wooden overhang. 'I thought they were all meant to be high-tailin' it out of here, not buying grub.'

'Look at all them goods them varmints have been buying,' Zack Nelson added pointing at the wagon. 'Where would dirt farmers get that kinda money?'

'They ain't both dirt farmers, boys,' Joe Conway muttered under his breath.

The two gunmen looked at Conway.

'What ya mean, Joe?' Nelson asked.

'Look at the shooting rig on the old guy,'

103

Conway observed. 'I never seen a dirt farmer with enough money to buy himself a hand-tooled shooting rig like that 'un. Whatever he is, he ain't no damn farmer.'

Both Cole and Nelson suddenly realized that their companion was right. The sun glinted off the pearl-handled grips as Dix tied down the boxes which were stacked high on the flatbed of the wagon.

'Who is he?'

'Reckon we ought to go ask him,' Conway said.

'He's trouble by the looks of it.'

Joe Conway spat at the ground. 'We can handle any trouble that he can dish out. Look at him. He's old. Real old.'

'But ordinary old men don't wear fancy shooting rigs like that, Joe,' Zack Nelson said.

Conway stepped closer to the edge of the boardwalk and squinted hard at the sight before them.

'I'd like to know what and who he is, Sam. And what he thinks he's doing in our valley helping a damn farmer.'

'What ya mean?' Cole adjusted his gunbelt and looked hard in the direction of the wagon.

'Joe means that although that critter has white hair, he must be darn good with them guns to have lived so long,' Zack Nelson explained.

'Yep. That ain't no ordinary drifter. That *hombre* is a gunfighter by the way those guns are hung on his hips,' Joe Conway said, rubbing his chin. 'He's even got them laced down to his thighs. Only men who are fast on the draw tie their holsters down that way.'

'What'll we do?' Nelson asked, knowing that he and his fellow gunslingers were far better at shooting people in the backs than at facing them.

Conway sighed heavily.

It was a good question and one that he did not have an answer for. He knew that he ought to ride back to Cal Harrigan and inform him about this man but his curiosity was burning at him. He wanted to know who it was who chose to side with one of the settlers.

'He makes me kinda curious.'

'We ain't thinking of going up to him, are we, Joe?' Cole asked nervously.

'That ain't the plan is it, Joe?' Nelson added.

'Hush up, boys. Let's go have us a confab with that gent.' Conway stepped down into the blazing sun and began to walk across the distance between themselves and the wagon outside the hardware store.

With Cole and Nelson flanking him, Conway closed in on the laden-down prairie schooner.

'We gonna have us a shoot out, Joe?' There was reluctance in the trembling voice.

'I reckon that the three of us ought to be able to get the better of an old critter like him,' Conway replied. He flicked the loops off his gun hammers and rested his gloved hands on top of the wooden gun grips.

Caleb Watkins placed the heavy sack of flour on

to the end of the wagon and stood watching the three approaching gunmen. He was about to say something to Dix but then noticed that his friend had already spotted them.

'I see them, Caleb.' Tom Dix walked carefully through the boxes and sacks on the flatbed of the wagon until he reached the tailgate. He dropped down on to the street and placed a hand on Caleb's shirt.

'Get inside the store.'

'But, Dix?' the farmer protested.

'Get inside the store now!' This time Dix's voice told the unarmed man that this was not a request. It was an order.

Joe Conway and his two companions fanned out a mere twenty feet from Dix. They stopped in their tracks and rested their hands on the grips of their weapons.

'Who are you, stranger?' Conway growled.

Dix studied the three men and felt his heart start to beat faster. He kept his hands at his sides and flexed his fingers.

'Who wants to know?'

Conway raised his chin and stared down his nose at the man before him. A man with hair that was the colour of snow. A man who looked far too old to be a threat. Yet there was no sign of fear in the voice of Dix.

'You like dying, old man?' Joe Conway could not understand why this man appeared to be unafraid. How many times had he faced three armed men before?

'I never tried it, sonny.' Dix smiled. 'But I have me a feeling that it'll take better men than you three to manage it.'

Conway raised his voice. 'You either answer my question or we'll send you to hell.'

Tom Dix laughed out loud. He had faced many men and heard every known threat in his time, but that was a new one.

'I've been to hell, boy. I spent twelve years there. What else have you got to threaten me with?'

Sam Cole and Zack Nelson began to move away from Joe Conway. They were trying to give their intended victim an impossible target to aim at.

Dix paid them no heed. He just stared straight at the face of the talkative Conway.

'I'll ask you again. Who are you, old-timer?' Joe Conway was now getting angry. He knew that most men shied away when faced with three gunmen, yet this man stood his ground and smiled.

'My name's Tom Dix.'

Conway spat at the ground between them.

'I never heard of you.'

Suddenly there was a voice behind Harrigan's three hired gunmen.

'Have you heard of me, sonny?'

Conway dragged a boot backwards and stared at the boardwalk in front of the café. The sight that he and then his two comrades spied, chilled them to their marrow.

Wild Bill Hickok was standing with the tails of his frock-coat pushed behind his narrow hips. His hands were held almost in prayer in front of the gun grips which poked out from the specially designed gunbelt.

Conway felt ice-cold sweat running down his face from beneath the hat-band of his Stetson. For the first time in all the days that he had plied his evil trade, he was caught between two men who looked like they knew how to use their guns.

'What do they call you, girlie?' Joe Conway shouted at Hickok. 'Am I meant to be afraid of someone with hair longer than my mother's?'

'He is kinda pretty except for the moustache.' Nelson laughed out loud.

The famous gunfighter stepped down into the street and began the long walk towards the three men.

'Did you just call Wild Bill Hickok a girl, boy?'

'Hickok?' Sam Cole repeated the name fearfully.

'Oh my dear Lord. That's Wild Bill Hickok.' Zack Nelson turned and ran for all his worth.

Terror overwhelmed Sam Cole. He watched as Nelson ran off and then glanced at Conway. He tried to lick his lips but there was no spittle in his mouth.

'You're Wild Bill Hickok?' Conway also vainly tried to swallow. 'I thought you were dead.'

Hickok stopped his advance and glared at the two men.

'Draw!' he shouted.

Cole started to run but Conway grabbed hold of

him and held him like a human shield between Hickok and himself.

Tom Dix walked to the side of the tall Hickok.

'I think we scared them enough, Bill.'

Wild Bill ignored Dix and took another step towardsthe two men and then shouted again.

'Draw!'

Conway held the struggling Cole in the grip of his left arm as his right hand went for his pistol. As the gun cleared its holster, he saw the famous cross-draw of Hickok in action.

Wild Bill drew both his weapons and aimed one at the pair of men in front of him and the other at the fleeing Nelson. Without a second's hesitation, he fired a single shot from both weapons.

Both bullets found their chosen targets.

Zack Nelson was felled as he reached their horses. Conway released his hold on Sam Cole and staggered backwards as he realized that Hickok's shot had gone straight through his throat and out of the back of his neck. Blood seemed to flood into his mouth. He tried to raise his gun again.

Hickok squeezed the trigger of the Colt in his left hand again and watched as Conway was lifted off the ground in a cloud of blood and gunsmoke.

Tom Dix stepped to the side of the tall man who was looking at Sam Cole angrily.

'It's over, Wild Bill. He ain't gonna draw on you.'

Hickok stared at Cole.

'Ride out of here, sonny. And remember that you're only alive because of my friend Tom Dix.'

The terrified gunman got to his feet and ran off towards where the three horses waited next to the body of Zack Nelson.

Wild Bill slid both guns into their holsters and then turned to look at Dix.

'Why did you kill them, Bill? They were no match for you.'

Hickok stared down his long narrow nose at the shorter man.

'Nobody makes fun of James Butler Hickok and lives to tell the tale, Dixie. Nobody.'

Tom Dix watched silently as the tall man walked towards a saloon.

# SIXTEEN

Enos White had listened to the words of Matt Blair for longer than most before he too walked out into the blazing sunshine and tried to get some fresh air into his cigar-smoke-filled lungs. He noticed Cal Harrigan brooding beside some of his men as soon as his ageing eyes adjusted to the light in the courtyard.

'I don't like none of this, Cal.'

'You got your orders straight, Enos?' Harrigan asked the red-faced rancher.

'That man is insane, Cal,' White whispered.

'Some of what he says might just work though,' Harrigan reluctantly admitted.

White nodded.

'That's the trouble. It does. But he's still as crazy as loco beans. I don't hanker after following the orders of a man who would kill all of us to make a point.'

'You gonna obey his orders?'

Enos White shrugged and glanced nervously

111

over his shoulder. 'I reckon I ought to. The alternative seems rather fatal.'

Suddenly the talking men gathered outside the large ranch house went silent as Blair walked out into the sunlight. His eyes flashed from one face to another as he searched for a hint of disobedience amongst their ranks. There was none. For brutal as the shootist was, he was capable of achieving what they had not been capable of.

Matt Blair knew how to kill every one of the settlers swiftly and neatly.

'I reckon you boys ain't used to taking orders, huh?' Blair said in a cold deliberate tone as he walked amongst them. All fifty plus of them moved out of his path like frightened children.

Matt Blair raised a hand to his eyes to shield them from the brilliant sunlight, and stared out at the horizon. He had spotted something that none of the gathered gunfighters had. He trained his eyes on the distant rising dust.

'There's a rider heading here real fast, Harrigan,' Blair announced coldly.

The rancher moved away from White and his men. He stood next to the shootist, screwed his eyes up and stared off into the heat haze.

'I see him.'

'Who is it?' White asked.

'Is it one of your boys?' Blair asked as his hands rested on the grips of his guns. 'If it's someone you want killing, I'm ready and willing.'

Harrigan said nothing as he watched the rider

galloping closer and closer. Whoever it was, he thought, he was whipping his horse savagely.

'Is it one of your men, Harrigan?' Matt Blair repeated his venomous question. Every one of the men around him could see that he was eager to kill, there and then. It was a habit that he had neglected for weeks and he wanted to refresh his taste for it.

Finally the rancher was able to identify the horseman.

'Yep. That's Sam Cole. He's one of my boys.'

Enos White looked hard into the face of Harrigan.

'What's wrong, Cal?'

'He's alone. He should be riding back with Joe and Zack. Why the hell is he on his own?'

Matt Blair watched the terrified rider galloping towards them.

'You say that he should be with two of your other boys, Harrigan?'

Harrigan was troubled. 'Yep.'

Cole rode into the courtyard, leapt from his mount and staggered up to his boss. He was panting like an old hound-dog as he reached the wide-shouldered man.

'We got us some trouble, Mr Harrigan.'

'What kinda trouble, Sam?'

'Them nesters have got themselves a couple of real useful friends,' Sam Cole gasped as he tried to get his second wind.

'What you talking about, boy?'

'Some gunfighter named Tom Dix and Wild Bill

Hickok stood up against me and the boys back at Hangman's Corner.'

Harrigan raised an eyebrow. 'I recall a critter named Dix from my rustling days. You say he's with Hickok?'

'Yep. They opened up on us when we was trying to get the better of one of them settlers.'

Matt Blair pulled the tight gloves over his hands.

'Are you sure it was Hickok?'

Cole looked into the deadly eyes of Blair. 'There ain't no mistaking that man. It was Wild Bill all right.'

'Where's Joe and Zack?' Harrigan asked holding the shoulders of the young gunman. 'Where are they, Sam?'

'Dead,' Sam Cole replied fearfully. 'They're both dead. Hickok killed them both. I never seen anyone draw as fast as that bastard did.'

'They're dead?' Harrigan repeated the word in disbelief. 'We better saddle up and ride to town and teach that Hickok a lesson.'

Blair exhaled a long line of smoke.

'No. We carry out my plan. The hooded riders will ride tonight and by morning there won't be a settler left in your valley, Harrigan.'

Cal Harrigan's head turned. There was fire in his face as he shouted.

'I want vengeance, mister. An eye for an eye. Hickok will pay dearly for killing my men. I don't care how good he is with his damn guns. He can't handle fifty men.'

114

Matt Blair gritted his teeth and stared back at the angry rancher.

'We destroy the settlers tonight,' he insisted.

'But we can't let Hickok get away with killing my men!'

'We won't.' Blair patted the face of the older man. 'I've waited five years to get a chance of going up against that long-haired dandy. He's mine!'

The men around the shootist watched as the tall lean figure walked back towards the house.

'Hickok is mine! Wild Bill Hickok dies tonight!

# SEVENTEEN

Tom Dix stood beside the unloaded wagon and stared off into the low sun. He knew that night was coming in fast and wondered what darkness might bring to this small homestead and the other similar ones dotted along the Pecos Valley.

'What's eatin' at you, Dixie?' Dan Shaw asked as he ambled across the yard towards his friend.

Dix looked at the retired lawman and pushed his hat up off his brow.

'You figure that those hooded riders will make an appearance tonight, Dan?' he asked.

Shaw shrugged and leaned on the side of the wagon.

'Maybe. The thing is, they got a lot of farms to choose from if they decide to attack.'

Dixie shook his head.

'They'll come looking for me.'

'How do you figure that, Dixie?'

'I was the one with Wild Bill when those two critters were killed.' Tom Dix looked at the stockpile of supplies he had paid for stacked up against the side of the tool-shack. There was enough there to last these poor people a year.

'But you told me that it was Wild Bill who shot those gunmen, not you,' Dan said.

'So?'

'And you stopped him from killing the third one,' Dan continued. 'You actually saved the third critter from meeting the same fate as his cohorts.'

'Yep.'

'Then it'll be more likely that they go to Hangman's Corner to get even with Bill, not here to kill you.'

Dix nodded as the logic of the words sank in. 'Then that means Wild Bill is in danger.'

'I reckon he's figured that out already and will be waiting for them, Dixie.'

Tom Dix looked at the scarlet embers spreading across the sky above them as the large sun slowly began to set.

'But Bill is more than able to handle anything that those ranchers' gunmen might throw at him,' Dan said.

'Unless they all ride in together after him, Dan.' Dixie sighed. 'Can Wild Bill Hickok cope with twenty or more gunmen at once?'

'If anyone can, it's James Butler Hickok.'

Dix nodded. 'Yeah. If anyone can. . . .'

Dan Shaw knew exactly what his partner was thinking. He wanted to ride to the assistance of their friend. Yet, to do so would be to leave Caleb,

118

Bessie and little Rosemary at the mercy of the hooded riders should they decide to strike once again. There were no easy answers to the problem that faced them.

'What'll we do, Dan?'

Dan bit his lip.

'I ain't got me no idea. You want to go and help Bill but you and me both know that we might be needed here. What can I say, Dixie? It's your call.'

Tom Dix pushed himself away from the wagon and looked at the small child innocently playing beside the stacked boxes. She was totally unaware of what might happen.

'Well?' Dan asked.

'We stay here!'

# EIGHTEEN

For more than five hours the patrol had weaved its way through the strange landscape. None of the riders had imagined that there could be so much land beyond the wide Pecos River. Slowly it had dawned on the commanding officer why this stretch of uncharted land was so valuable to those who wished to control it. This was not a mere tract of land, this was a country.

Whoever controlled its rolling ranges, had power.

The army major knew that men would fight to the death to keep their hands on far smaller places than this. No wonder the people who had conquered this vast land totally rejected the law and everything it stood for and were determined to keep this all for themselves.

Major Harry Travis had quickly noticed that this was a land of many contrasts. Dry arid desert to the north, where the troop of soldiers had crossed into it, changing to a fertile lush range the further south they rode.

They had expected to find a normal valley that had rolling hills to both sides, but the Pecos was unlike any valley that any of the troopers had ever seen before. The further they rode into it, the more they began to wonder just how immense it could actually be.

The almost flat range appeared to go on for ever, the heat haze masking the hills which the army patrol knew had to be out there somewhere to the west. The troop had continued riding for hours and yet they had not seen any sign of life. Yet again, this was even more evidence of the sheer size of the lawless land.

Even darkness could not stop the patrol on its relentless exploration.

Major Travis stopped his two columns of troopers and waited until the burly Olaf Svenson drew his horse alongside the black charger. Both men were exhausted.

'Look, Sergeant,' Travis said pointing at the glowing lights below their high vantage point, 'what is that?'

Svenson stood in his stirrups and looked down from the dark ridge at the sight of the flames that twisted through the blackness below them.

'I reckon that's a lotta riders, sir.'

'Indeed, but what are they doing?' Travis knew that this was the last thing he had expected to find. 'And why are they carrying torches?'

'Maybe this is their way, sir.' Svenson shrugged as he rested his wide rump on the saddle.

'I don't like the look of it. There has to be at least fifty riders down there and they're all carrying torches.' The major rubbed his chin thoughtfully. 'We have to ask ourselves, who are they and where are they going?'

'And why,' the sergeant added.

'Exactly. Why?'

Sven eased his horse forward slightly. 'So far we ain't found any of them settlers you reckoned was over here, sir. I've got me a bad taste in my mouth. What if them riders are headed to the small homesteads to give them a surprise.'

Major Travis had been thinking the same thing.

'You must be a mind-reader, Olaf. I was thinking exactly the same thing.'

The sergeant patted Major Travis on his back.

'Ain't very hard to read the mind of any cavalry officer with a few gold bars on his shoulders, sir.'

'Whoever they are, they outnumber us,' Travis remarked.

'But they ain't soldiers like my little boys, Major,' Svenson gruffed. 'Them's civilians. Takes a dozen of them to handle one of my young 'uns.'

The major sighed and looked over his shoulder. 'Some of those boys are older than I am, Sergeant.'

'I reckon you might be right,' Svenson agreed. 'But they ain't weighed down by the pressures of command like you.'

Travis allowed his mount to carry on down the slope in the same direction in which the riders seemed to be heading.

'I think that the settlers must be due south, Sergeant. Let's go take a look.'

Olaf Svenson waved his arm at the troopers behind them and spurred his horse on after the tail of the magnificent charger. He knew only too well that they were headed into trouble. His experienced nostrils could smell it. Whoever they were who were carrying those fiery torches, they would not take kindly to the interference of an army troop.

The twenty-five cavalrymen rode down into the darkness with only the light of the moon to guide them on their way. They could see roughly where the riders with the torches were heading and Travis had instinctively worked out a route that ought to intercept them.

As they rode on towards the unknown, they spotted flames reaching up into the black sky about five miles ahead. Something was on fire and it was not brush. Gathering pace, Travis and his men heard gunshots echoing around the valley.

'Come on, men,' the major shouted out, gripping his reins in his gauntlets.

If the Devil himself had chosen to ride out of the fiery bowels of Hell, he could not have looked more imposing. Matt Blair had ensured that the ranchers and their hired hands all wore hoods before setting out from Harrigan's place.

All rode through the darkness carrying flaming torches in their gloved hands. Fifty-three horsemen galloped across the vast expanse of fertile range with one single thought filling their minds. To rid the valley of the settlers who were fencing off one section after another.

The men had already tasted the innocent blood of their victims and the acrid aroma of smoke lingered in their nostrils.

Now they would not stop until they had burned the last of the settlers' small homes to the ground. Nothing else would satisfy the riders who followed Matt Blair's galloping mount.

So far they had burned three of the small homesteads to the ground and made sure that they had killed every man, woman and child who had escaped the flames.

The sound of the gunfire still seemed to be ringing in their ears as they rode on. They were heading to the next small farm with their torches held high. The night was still young and they knew that they had more than enough time to destroy them all before dawn.

Matt Blair rode at the head of the hooded riders. The chambers of his sixguns were red hot. He had slain most of the settlers himself this night and wanted to kill more.

For he was the shootist.

# NINETEEN

One by one the small homes of the settlers were being put to the torch. The two men had watched helplessly for nearly an hour as the flames licked into the cloudless night sky, sending the stench of burning wood and human flesh drifting through the valley. Tom Dix and Dan Shaw stood beside the corral where their nervous horses pawed at ground with their hoofs. The animals could smell the death that lingered on the foul-smelling smoke.

The keen-eyed Dix could make out at least six individual blazes. The closer they were to the Watkins farm, the bigger the fire appeared.

Caleb and his wife had gone to their bed more than two hours earlier, long before the hooded riders had started their burning and killing.

Dix had brought both their Winchesters from their saddles and stood next to his friend watching in horror as the distant flames grew ever closer. Both men were fully armed and ready for whatever the night would bring.

127

'Can you make them out, Dixie?' Dan asked.

'Yep. I can see the bastards,' Dix drawled in his low Texan way. 'They're getting closer. I reckon that they'll try and finish it tonight, partner. They got themselves the taste of it in their mouths. Men are mighty dangerous when they got the taste in their damn mouths.'

Dan glanced at the brooding man. 'Taste of what?'

'Slaughter, *amigo*. Damn merciless slaughter.'

The sound of people screaming mixed with the gunfire on the night air. With every beat of the two men's hearts, the hooded riders drew closer. Soon, even Dan Shaw's eyes were capable of making out the dozens of blazing torches held by the insatiable riders.

'How close do you reckon they are, Dixie?' Dan asked as he rested the rifle on the top pole of the corral fence.

Dix bit at his lip.

'Too close, *amigo*. Too damn close.'

'They're burning and killing like maniacs.' Dan felt a cold shiver trace his spine. 'Why?'

Dix glanced through the moonlight at the troubled face of the retired law officer. It was a good face. An honest one that even now after all these years, could not understand the evil that lurks in so many men's ambitious souls.

'I reckon they just want to rid the Pecos of these poor critters, Dan.'

'It don't make no sense to me, Dixie,' Dan said

as he stared along the barrel of his carbine through the raised sights.

'Maybe that's why we get on so well, Dan. I don't trust hardly anybody and you trust every man you meet.'

'What you talking about?'

There was no time to reply.

Suddenly against the flaming backdrop of the distant fiery outrages, the two men could see figures coming across the fields towards them. Dix cranked the mechanism of his Winchester and brought it up to his shoulder.

'Who are they?' Dan whispered.

'We'll find out real soon,' Dixie answered as he stared down the length of his carbine's barrel. Then he heard a sound which made him feel sick. He lowered his rifle and listened again.

The sound of terror filled both men's ears.

These were not the cowardly vermin who hid their faces beneath hoods. These were frightened men, women and children fleeing for their very lives before the hooded riders reached their homesteads.

'Farmers!' Dan Shaw sighed.

Dix indicated for Dan to lower his rifle. 'Yep. And they're scared. Mighty scared.'

Both men heard the door of the house beside them opening and saw the troubled expressions of Caleb and Bessie illuminated by a single candle in the female's shaking hand.

'What's going on, Dixie?' the soft voice asked.

129

'We was woken up by noises. What's happening?'

Tom Dix ran to the open doorway.

'The hooded riders are on the rampage, ma'am,' Dix started. 'I think that a lot of your neighbours are headed here before they get themselves killed as well.'

Bessie looked up at her husband's face.

'We must try and give them shelter, Caleb.'

'You're right, dear.' Caleb squeezed his wife's shoulders and then leaned toward Dix. 'I'll get my britches and boots on. I'll be out in a minute, Dixie.'

Tom Dix turned and walked back towards Dan. He was becoming increasingly worried. He knew how to fight and had never considered his own welfare when standing up against his enemies, but there seemed to be dozens of figures moving across the ploughed field towards the Watkins farm.

True to his word, Caleb came out of the house less than a minute after he had spoken to the concerned Dix. No sooner had the farmer reached the fence than the first of Caleb's neighbours staggered up to them.

'Caleb?' a pitiful voice called out from the darkness.

'I'm here, friend,' Caleb responded.

A half-dozen figures staggered towards the three men near the corral gate. For a moment their terrified eyes fixed on the two strangers standing next to Caleb.

An elderly man pointed.

'Who is that with ya?'

'Come on. These are my friends,' the farmer told his fellow settlers. 'They're on our side.'

Reassured, the people advanced. The steady stream of men, women and children of all ages flowed through the gate to be greeted by Bessie. One family after another. Dix said nothing as the flood of scared faces passed by him. Most were still in their night-clothes and few had anything resembling weapons. He watched silently as the growing crowd grew to more than a hundred behind him.

The sound of hysterical sobbing was almost deafening.

So many targets for the hooded riders to aim their weapons at, Dix thought. So many innocent targets.

Dan touched Dix's elbow and pointed at the sight of yet another farmhouse erupting into flames as the hooded riders struck again.

'Look, Dixie!'

'I see it.' Tom Dix inhaled deeply and could taste the smoke in his dry mouth. As far as he could see in the moonlight, there were only three farms left untouched between the riders and themselves.

No more than two miles.

'What's eatin' you, Dixie?' Dan asked as he saw the look on his partner's face, a look which he had never seen before.

Dix raised an eyebrow at his pal. 'We have to try

and get these folks away from here, Dan. And we ain't got a lot of time to do it in before those riders get here.'

'You reckon?'

'Yep. I reckon,' Dix confirmed solidly. 'But first I want you to get every man here to douse the shingles on the roof of Caleb's house with water from the well. A wet roof won't burn.'

Dan Shaw nodded.

# TWENTY

Tom Dix stood totally alone in the small yard. He clutched the rifle across his chest and wondered how long it would take for Dan to return from the dense brushland that fringed the river. He had managed to talk his partner into shepherding the Watkins and their neighbours as far away from the small homestead as possible.

'Where the hell are you, Dan?' Dix whispered under his breath as he stared at the awesome riders.

The man who had once been a famed gunfighter knew that he still had all the skills of his former profession, yet this was not like anything Dix had ever faced before.

This was no showdown. This had the potential of becoming a massacre and he knew that it was doubtful if he would survive without Dan to back him up.

His eyes narrowed. He could see the riders heading straight towards him beneath the light of the moon. They had destroyed all the small homes further north and it was the turn of the Watkins place now. Dix knew that once they had razed this homestead to the ground the hooded riders would continue on south, killing and burning what remained of the settlers and their properties.

The inferno behind the riders gave them an almost nightmarish appearance. He pushed the rifle lever down quickly and drew it back until he heard the Winchester mechanism locking.

Dix drew the long rifle up and carefully tucked its wooden stock into the soft cushion of his shoulder. He knew that he had fourteen shots in the rifle before he would have to reload, but there would be no time to feed bullets into the gleaming rifle magazine once the riders arrived.

Once the shooting started and his trusty carbine was out of shells, he knew that he would have to rely upon the primed Colt .45s in his holsters. Fourteen and twelve, he thought. Twenty-six bullets and there had to be more than fifty riders heading straight at him through the smoke, with their blazing torches raised above their heads.

Dix checked his gunbelt and knew that he had fewer than twenty bullets there if he had time to reload. Even if he hit every target that he trained his weapons on, he knew that he was in trouble.

He desperately needed more bullets. Dix knew that he had two boxes of shells in his saddle-bags.

His eyes darted along the fence poles and he made the decision that he would leave the relative safety of his place of cover and attempt to reach them.

Tom Dix crouched down and moved along the length of the fence towards the rear of the corral. The mules and his mount were skittish already and could sense the impending doom.

Suddenly the ground around him erupted as bullets tore up its surface. It sounded as if every one of the riders had unleashed their lethal lead at his heels. A million blinding granules of dust showered over Dix. He spun around and fired the rifle before leaping over the stacked boxes of provisions. Dix landed hard and felt his age screaming at him to stop. He knew that he was no longer a young man as he crawled back on to his knees. Every bone in his body felt as though it had broken with the impact of his hitting the hard ground.

Faster than he had ever done before, Dix cranked the rifle lever again, aimed and fired, then ducked. He had seen his shot take a rider off his horse but now the boxes were being reduced to mere splinters.

It was as if every one of the hooded riders' weapons were trained on him. Smouldering wood fragments showered over him as he crawled away. He had timed this all wrong, he thought.

Dix cranked his rifle once more.

He was seeking shadows but could not find any.

Blazing torches came crashing over his head. Dozens of them lighting up every single shadow of darkness that he was trying to use for cover.

It sounded like a hundred thunderstorms. The night air exploded as countless rifle and pistol bullets rained down on the tool-shack as Dix deperately crawled around the back of its fragile walls.

Then as he managed to find a gap in the wall which he might use to aim his rifle through, he saw more blazing torches landing inside the shack.

The hay on the floor of the crude structure burst violently into flames inside the shack, causing Dix to fall backwards. He realized that his rifle barrel had caught on the ragged wooden wall. Dix tried to pull his weapon free but the tinder-dry shack turned into a white-hot wall of fire.

Then he heard the riders circling to his left.

'There he is,' one of the hooded men called from the back of his horse.

'Kill him!' Dix heard another voice ordering.

Without even thinking, he pulled both his guns free of their holsters and fired. He hit one rider and then another. Then he felt a bullet skimming his ribs.

For the first time in his entire life, he felt panic filling him like a poison. He looked to his left and then to his right, trying to work out which way offered the safest route away from the blazing shack.

Then he heard another volley of bullets.

This time they had fired straight at the walls of flaming wooden boards.

Slivers of flame ripped from the white-hot wall.

It was like a score of fire arrows tearing through the night air at him. Dix ran up into the dense brush for all he was worth.

Somehow, for the first time in years, he was running like a man half his age. He had to. There were still far too many of them and they had the advantage.

Dix fired behind him at the sound of the yelling riders. He knew that he had hit some of them by the time both his guns were empty, but he continued running.

The only thing that could save him now was darkness.

Total darkness.

Dix could feel a pain in his side with every step as the bullets continued to cut through the air around him. He knew that one of the bullets had taken a chunk out of his ribs and blood was flowing down his side, yet Dix still moved quickly as he ducked and swayed through the undergrowth.

There was no time to think about anything except getting out of the range of the rifles and guns that were trained on him. He knew that if he could just keep moving there was a slim chance that he could find a place where he could reload his Colts and then head back in on the hooded riders.

Finally he saw it.

A shallow ditch between two tall trees beckoned and he did not ignore it.

Tom Dix threw himself down into the hole.

Before he had time to shake the spent shells from his guns he heard a handful of the hooded riders charging after him. He rolled up against the wall of the ditch and watched as the six riders spurred their horses over him.

# TWENTY-ONE

Dix lay on his side and reloaded the pistols as quickly as he could. His fingers checked the gunbelt ammunition loops and found that there were three bullets remaining after he had closed the chambers of his guns.

His mind raced.

Dix knew that there were at least forty-five hooded riders back at the small courtyard of the Watkins homestead searching the brush for him. He hoped that they would not find the innocent farmers and their families instead.

He heard the gunfire again. At least a half dozen shots rang through the night air. This time it was coming from the direction of the river.

He began to fear the worst.

Dix rose to his feet, stared over the top of the ditch and tried to see. But even the moon could not penetrate through the dense tree canopy above him.

He wondered where the six riders had gone. He

prayed it was not in the same direction as Dan had led the scores of settlers. Yet in his heart, he knew that was exactly where the shots had come from.

Shots rang out in the darkness again.

Tom Dix clambered out from the ditch and pulled back his gun hammers until he felt them locking. He feared that Dan had ridden straight into the barrels of the hooded riders. If he had, Dix knew that it would be his fault.

Dan Shaw had only entered the infamous Pecos Valley because of him.

Dix heard something straight ahead. It was the hooded riders' horses returning. When he went to walk towards the sound he felt an agonizing pain which stopped him in his tracks. He leaned against the largest of the trees and waited. Dix could feel the blood running from the raw wound in his side and knew that he would have to try and finish off the horsemen as soon as they rode into view.

He gritted his teeth and tried to ignore the pain as the sound of the horses grew louder and louder. Sweat trailed down his face as he somehow managed to convince himself that he was not really injured at all. All the years he had spent in a chain gang had taught him that it was possible to find a place in his mind where pain did not exist.

It was how he had survived.

Tom Dix took a deep breath and held his weapons at arm's length, watching the brush ahead of him. He was ready to fire when suddenly a few spooked horses came thundering out of the bushes and galloped passed him.

The wide-eyed horses had lost their masters.

Dix lowered his guns in confusion.

Then he heard another horse coming towards him at pace. He raised the Colts again and steadied himself. The horse came through the brush fast and startled Dix. Just as his fingers were about to squeeze on the triggers of his Colts, his keen eyes recognized the familiar face of the rider.

Dan Shaw reined in hard. He pulled up beside his wounded companion.

'You OK, Dixie?' Dan asked as he watched his friend stagger back until the tree stopped his retreat. He did not wait for an answer and dismounted quickly.

Dix felt his friend's hands gripping at his shoulders.

'I thought those killers must have got you for sure, Dan.'

'I got them first, Dixie,' Dan said. He pulled his canteen from the saddle and gave his friend a drink of the cold liquid.

Dixie rubbed his mouth dry on the back of his sleeve and stared hard at the man beside him. 'How did you get the better of six hooded riders, Dan? When have you ever hit what you've aimed at?'

'You think that I ain't learned nothing from being with you, Dixie?' Dan Shaw screwed the stopper back on his canteen and returned it to the saddle horn. 'I ain't such a bad shot.'

141

'What really happened, you old liar?' Dix managed to smile through his pain as he walked to the horse and leaned against it.

Shaw shrugged. 'Hell, you can be kinda hard on a man's pride, Dixie. The truth is that they came galloping at me and I just started shooting with both my guns. I figure they didn't see me too well 'cos of them hoods they was wearing. I managed to pick the six of them off before they even spotted me.'

Dix nodded.

'That I believe.'

Dan Shaw suddenly noticed his pal's blood-soaked side. He tried to check the wound. Dix pushed him away.

'It ain't that bad, Dan. We've got work to finish.'

The retired lawman knew better than to argue with his friend when he was hurt. 'How many of the bastards are left back there, Dixie?'

'Maybe forty.'

Dan shook his head. 'Too many. That's way too many.'

'We've got to stop them, Dan. There ain't nobody else to stop them except us. The trouble is we need more ammunition.'

A broad smile spread across Dan's face. 'I've got me plenty of that and a lot more besides.'

Dix stared at his pal.

'What ya mean?' Dix asked as he watched his friend pointing to the scabbard beneath his saddle. There were three Winchesters rammed into the gap between the blanket and the cinch straps.

'Those riders dropped them and I picked them up, Dixie.'

'You did fine. Now we got us some power.'

'What do we do now?' Dan asked.

'First you help me get on to this nag of yours and then we'll ride a half-mile north and circle back in on Caleb's place,' Dix replied. He began doing up the brass studs of his jacket until it was tight around his middle. The rough material pressed at the wound hard enough for him not to be able to feel it bleeding.

'Can we take on forty of them, Dixie?' Dan asked as he undid the buckle on his saddle-bag.

'Well at least we've got enough bullets now,' Dix answered, as his friend helped him mount the horse and then handed him a box of bullets from his saddle-bag.

Dan stepped into the stirrup and climbed up behind his pal.

'That ain't what I asked.'

'I know,' Dix said spurring the horse on.

# TWENTY-TWO

Matt Blair had ripped his hood from his head minutes earlier when he had realized that he was losing men for the first time that night. He was angry. More angry than he had ever been during his long infamous career. The shootist hauled back on his reins and tossed his blazing torch on to the roof of Caleb Watkins's small house. To his amazement it, like all the others, did not ignite the wet wooden shingles.

'Get coal-oil from someplace, boys!' he yelled at the top of his voice. He would not be defeated by what he regarded as simple-minded people. 'No nesters are gonna get the better of us. This shack is gonna go up in flames.'

Cal Harrigan rode up beside the furious horseman and dragged off his own crude hood.

'Who the hell was that shooting at us, Mr Blair?' he asked, keeping a short rein on the neck of his nervous horse.

Blair spun his horse full circle on a tight leather

and studied the area that surrounded them.

'I got me a glimpse of that bastard's face. I reckon it was the sidewinder called Tom Dix,' the shootist replied.

'Who is Tom Dix?' Harrigan asked as their riders rode around the confined area trampling the crops beneath the hoofs of their horses.

'A low-down Texan,' Blair growled. 'I only seen him in action once when I was a kid. He can be a real pain in the saddle.'

Both men looked around them again. They had not made a lot of difference to this place, unlike all the others they had raided that night. Apart from burning the tool-shed to the ground, they had not managed to continue their ruthless killing spree.

After riding in to the second small settlement, they had not even seen a human being as they had destroyed the last five homesteads. The sheer ferocity of their savagery had alerted everyone to what was happening. Their intended victims had fled long before Matt Blair and his followers had reached their properties.

'What would Tom Dix be doing here?' Harrigan asked, keeping his skittish mount close to the powerful horse of the angry shootist.

'I ain't seen or heard of him in more than twenty years, Harrigan.' Blair rubbed his neck. 'The thing is that he's here and that can only spell trouble for the likes of us.'

'Are you worried by this Dix *hombre*?' Cal Harrigan made the mistake of asking.

'There ain't a man alive that I'm afraid of,' Blair snarled through the smoke-filled air that drifted across the Watkins place. The problem was, Blair had already seen four of his riders shot by a man he knew had to be the famous Tom Dix. He had sent a half-dozen riders chasing him up into the dense brush at the back of the homestead and heard shots ringing out in the darkness, but he knew that men like Dix did not die easily.

'Look!' Harrigan pointed past the burning tool-shack. 'I see horses coming back.'

Blair spat at the ground and focused on the riderless horses galloping out of the brush. His worst fears had been right. Tom Dix could not be killed so easily.

It was all going wrong and he knew it.

Harrigan turned his mount and stared into the face that was illuminated by the distant flames along the range. He could see the anger and confusion etched on it.

'I reckon we ought to quit. Let's light out of here and head back to my place and . . .'

'You trying to give the orders now, old man?' Blair screamed out.

'No, but things are going belly-up.'

'I give the orders around here!' Blair jabbed his spurs into the flesh of his mount, pulled back hard on his horse's neck and forced it to rear up. With perfect balance, Blair hung on to his reins and encouraged his horse to kick out with its hoofs at Harrigan.

This mount was as evil as its master and seemed to relish striking out like a cornered mustang at the shocked rancher.

Harrigan tried to shield himself but felt the metal horseshoes hitting him hard to his body and then his head. He tried to urge his horse away but it stumbled, sending him crashing down on to the churned-up ground.

Enos White rode close with his own hired men but neither said or did anything to the shootist.

Matt Blair laughed at the moon and allowed his horse to settle once more. His cold brutal eyes watched as the other riders gathered all around him. Their eyes glared through the holes in their hoods at the vicious shootist. But not one of them dared to say anything to Blair. For they feared him and he seemed to fear nothing at all.

But even frightened men reach a point where they can no longer hide away beneath the hoods of cowardice. Enos White steered his horse closer to his fallen associate and the deadly shootist.

'What you do that for, Blair? You crazy or something?' White screamed at the grim-faced rider.

Without a second thought, Matt Blair swiftly drew both his guns and fired two shots.

The first took White off the back of his grey mare and the second hit Harrigan before he could get back up off the ground.

Both shots were deadly accurate.

'Looks like a lot of you boys have a new boss. And I seem to have inherited a whole lot of land

and wealth from our deceased friends,' Blair gloated as he wondered how much money his victims might have been worth before their sudden spiral into the bowels of hell.

There was a stunned silence amongst the gathered gunmen and remaining ranchers. They stared in disbelief as Blair rode through their ranks towards the house that refused to burn. He pulled his horse's head back hard, stood in his stirrups and suddenly pointed his right gun.

'Look, men!'

The reluctant gunmen eased their mounts forward and stared out to where their brutal leader was aiming his still-smoking pistol. None of them uttered a word. They dared not open their mouths for fear of his killing them as swiftly as he had killed White and Harrigan.

The large moon betrayed Tom Dix and Dan Shaw, who were riding to the north of the homestead atop the exhausted mount.

'Can you see them? They must be the swine who've been killing our riders.' Matt Blair could feel the hatred of the silent horsemen behind him. As he spun his mount around something else caught his attention.

A haunting cavalry bugle rang out through the smoke.

The sound of the bugle alerted the hooded riders around the shootist that the army was heading towards them along their precious Pecos Valley.

149

'Soldiers!' a voice amongst the horsemen exclaimed.

The few remaining ranchers began shouting orders to their gunfighters as Matt Blair moved his horse closer to the long fence poles.

'What the hell is the army doing here? This is free range. There ain't no law here,' he screamed loudly as he spotted the twenty-five troopers charging along the range towards him and his hooded followers. 'There ain't no law west of the Pecos River.'

Then his eyes spotted the horse carrying the two riders closing in on the Watkins place.

It was Tom Dix!

Turning the tall horse around, the shootist noticed that more than half of the hooded riders had already fled the small Watkins courtyard, and were scattering over the vast smoke-filled valley. Those remaining of the gunfighters who had belonged to either Enos White or Cal Harrigan seemed unable to know what they should do next. They were helpless to do anything except remain with the deadly shootist. But there were only about twelve of them left.

Suddenly the tables had been turned and it was he who was outnumbered and outgunned.

'We'll head back to Harrigan's place and then on to White's, boys,' Blair shouted from the back of his mount.

Then red-hot tapers rained through the night air around the hooded riders. Blair heard the sound of gunfire filling the air behind him.

These were not the bullets of his hooded riders, he thought. These were the bullets of the cavalry troop and Dix. And they were aimed at him and what remained of his followers. The hound had suddenly become the fox.

And the fox did not like it one bit.

With bullets speeding through the air like a swarm of deadly fireflies, Matt Blair dug in his spurs and drove his mount mercilessly away from the homestead. He waved at the dozen remaining hooded riders to follow him as he galloped out of the yard.

They did.

The shootist gazed to his right. It was Dix who was closest. He could see the now aged face clearly as he headed off into the open range.

As the twelve riders rode out on to the moonlit range, a volley of shots rained into their ranks from the guns of Tom Dix and the single-shot Springfield rifles of the trailing cavalry troop.

The chilling sound of wounded horses hung sickeningly on the smoke-filled air.

Two of the horses closest to that of Matt Blair were cut down by the volley of bullets. As they fell, the trailing mounts either pulled up or crashed over them. Hooded men flew through the air and landed heavily. The sound of bones breaking was everywhere.

Tom Dix hauled back on his reins with one hand and kept a pistol trained at the pile of human and

151

equine bodies strewn out before them. Dan Shaw quickly slid off the back of the mount and pulled one of the Winchester rifles out from beneath his saddle. He cranked the mechanism and aimed it at the stunned riders as they tried to stagger to their feet.

'You better not move an inch, boys.' Dan warned the hooded riders at his feet. 'I'll kill the lot of you if you try to stand or go for your guns.'

Dix heard the thundering hoofs behind him and turned his head slightly to look at the troopers. Then he looked out at the rider who was galloping away from them. A rider who was out of range and yet still whipping his mount for all he was worth.

'Who is that yella bastard?' Dix asked the men on the ground.

'Matt Blair,' a feeble defeated voice replied.

Dan looked at Dix who was still holding the reins in one hand and a gun in the other.

'You heard of him, Dixie?'

'Yep.' Dix spat at the ground. 'He's a low-life maniac. He's a so called shootist.'

By the time the words sank into Dan's tired brain, Major Travis and his two columns of troopers had pulled up beside Dix and Shaw. The soldiers began dismounting.

Travis stared at the hooded riders in total disbelief. He still could not believe the horrors he had witnessed during the past few hours, but before he could ask any of the vermin at his feet a single question, one of them pulled a gun and fired wildly at the mounted men above him.

Major Travis had only just felt the heat of the bullet passing his face when he was deafened by the shot that came from beside him.

A shot that entered the crude cloth hood of the gunman below them and blew the hidden head apart. The cavalry officer turned and looked at Tom Dix, who sat silently holding one of his Colt .45s in his hand. Smoke drifted from the barrel into the moonlight.

'Thank you, mister.' Travis sighed.

Tom Dix nodded and then stood in his stirrups. 'You see what I see?'

The unmistakable figure of James Butler Hickok was heading at an even pace straight toward them from the direction of Hangman's Corner. With a style that few men ever lived long enough to perfect, Hickok eased his mount to a halt beside Tom Dix and the army officer.

'Is it all over, Dixie?' Hickok asked as his hooded eyes stared at the men who were being shackled by the soldiers.

'The leader rode off in that direction, Wild Bill.' Dix sighed as he slid his Colt into its holster and turned the horse around to face the wide open range.

'What was his name?' Hickok chewed on the end of an unlit cigar before striking a match with his thumbnail and sucking in its flame.

'These wretches said his name was Matt Blair.' Tom Dix answered.

The smoke drifted from the mouth of the famous horseman as he touched the brim of his John B. Stetson at the cavalry officer and turned his own horse.

'The shootist,' Wild Bill Hickok said. 'He's been wanting to meet me for a long while. Reckon it's time I obliged.'

Suddenly both Dix and Hickok jabbed their spurs and galloped off across the moonlit range after the evil rider. The dust from Blair's horse's hoofs still lingered.

It was an easy trail to follow.

# FINALE

Tom Dix and Wild Bill Hickok knew that the large moon above them made them an easy target as they thundered on towards the large ranch house and outbuildings, yet they did not slow their pace or seek cover. The dust left by the hoofs of the shootist's mount still hung a few feet above the ground and led straight beneath the imposing sign which read simply HARRIGAN.

As both riders drew closer, they could make out the lathered-up horse tied to a hitching rail outside the huge house with its door flung wide open.

Blair was inside and busy.

So busy that he had no time to look over his shoulder at who or what might have trailed him to this place.

It was Hickok who first eased his reins back and slowed the tall horse to walking pace. Dix followed suit. Both riders stopped their mounts at the sign above them and then dismounted.

Hickok's face appeared like a stone statue in the eerie light of the moon as he tied his reins around one of the wooden sign uprights. Tom Dix studied the tall man who removed his hat and hung it by its drawstring over the saddle horn. He had never understood the complex character but had probably come closer than most.

Dix emptied the spent shells from the chambers of his guns and carefully reloaded them from the box that Dan had given him earlier. The few remaining bullets were slid into the empty loops on his gunbelt before he snapped the chambers shut and spun them.

Dix pulled back on the hammers of his trusty weapons and felt them both locking into position. For every action he had taken, Hickok had just stood silently staring at the open doorway of the house.

Wild Bill had earned the name long ago for a very good reason that few had ever challenged. His mood could change in a mere heartbeat.

'You going to check them irons of yours, Bill?' Dix asked as he walked to the side of the man whose long brown hair floated on the gentle night breeze behind his broad back.

'No need, Dixie,' Hickok said.

Both men began walking towards the house at an even pace. The long thin legs of the taller man took one stride to every two of Tom Dix's.

'What do you reckon he's doing in there, Wild Bill?'

'Stealing every damn cent he can lay his grubby hands on, I reckon,' Hickok replied without taking his eyes off the open doorway.

Dix knew that his friend had only one thing on his mind and it was not idle conversation. For some reason, all the famous gunfighter could think about was killing the shootist. Dix wondered what spurred a man like Hickok on. He had nothing left to prove and yet he continued placing himself at risk.

'You don't like this Blair *hombre*. Why?'

'He's a shootist. That's reason enough,' Hickok said in a way that ended the small talk between them.

Then both men stopped in their tracks. They could hear movement inside the large unlit house. Suddenly Matt Blair came through the open doorway with a canvas bag in his arms. His eyes widened as he saw Dix and Hickok standing a mere twenty feet before him.

In one flowing movement, Matt Blair dropped the heavy bag and went for his guns.

Wild Bill jumped to his right and hit Tom Dix off his feet and then moved his slim fingers over the grips of his pistols. As Dix hit the ground and rolled over, he saw the famous cross-draw skill of his tall friend in action.

Both barrels of Hickok's guns came curling around as his thumbs pulled the hammers back.

Before Matt Blair had even managed to get his own weapons clear of his holsters, Hickok's fingers had pulled back on the triggers. The two shots deafened the stunned onlooker.

Holding on to his own primed Colts Tom Dix watched Matt Blair's lifeless body lift off the ground as the two bullets entered him dead centre.

The man was thrown into the wall behind him by the sheer force of the deadly impact of Hickok's bullets. As the empty shell that had once been Matt Blair slid down the wall, a crimson line of blood remained on the plastered surface.

Tom Dix got to his feet, released the hammers on his guns and holstered them. He watched the long-haired man silently straighten up to his full height.

Hickok twirled both weapons on his slender fingers until both the guns ended up in their hand-tooled holsters.

Dix watched as his friend turned and began walking towards their horses. It was as if nothing had happened.

'You OK, Bill?' Dix asked as he caught up with the taller figure.

Hickok did not answer until he reached his waiting horse. He plucked his Stetson off the horn of the saddle and placed it on his head and then untied the reins. Only as he placed a boot into the stirrup and glided up on to the back of his tall mount, did he look at his old friend.

'I'm OK, Dixie. But you're wounded.'

'It's just a flesh wound.' Tom Dix mounted his tired horse and sat looking at the brooding figure. He was about to speak when the living legend sighed heavily and pulled out a cigar from his deep jacket pocket. Dix watched as his pal bit off the tip of the cigar and then gripped it between his teeth.

'That man was pure evil, Dixie,' Wild Bill said.

'I know, Wild Bill. I know.'

'Reckon there will be peace in the Pecos now.' Wild Bill Hickok shrugged as he struck a match with his thumbnail and lit the cigar in his mouth.

'And law,' Dix added. They both started their horses on the return journey.

Hickok laughed as smoke drifted from his mouth.

'There will be law west of the Pecos. I don't like the sound of that, Dixie. Folks will blame us for that.'

Tom Dix stood in his stirrups and allowed the horse beneath him to find its own pace.

'You could be right.'

Hickok stood in his own stirrups and let his tall stallion gather speed. 'I guess that means we'll have to get old Dan out of his rocking-chair and try and find us another place to live. We ain't the sort who get on in those modern civilized places.'

'Reckon so, James Butler.'

The two horses thundered across the wide range beneath the large moon.

It was over.